Something Like A House

'A work that is dense with politics, history and science, but which has a ring of absolute truth. It reads not so much as a novel about an experience but as one that renders the experience itself – startling, strange, unmediated'

Melissa Denes, *Daily Telegraph*

'An unsentimental exploration of the privations of peasant life, a horrifyingly dispassionate portrayal of the brutal farce that was the Cultural Revolution and a clinical dissection of the racial insecurity that has informed the Chinese psyche. The beauty of the author's approach is the way in which he subverts our sensibilities through stealth, using language to tease wisps of mist across meaning, forcing us to look more carefully, forcing us to consider nuances that may ordinarily have passed us by. The result is a book that eats away at your heart whilst challenging our very understanding of what a novel should be'

Birmingham Post

'It is an impressively well-researched and sensitively imagined picture of an almost unknown society . . . told in haunting, piercingly spare prose which never fails to make an impact'

Anthea Lawson, *The Times*

'A marvellous terseness, a stark, brilliant poetry . . . a gripping literary thriller'

Peter Ho Davies, *Independent*

'A wholly convincing account that wears its research lightly, portraying both the cycles of rural life and the upheavals of revolution with impressive economy. History and its horrors are not the only features of this mysterious and occasionally lyrical novel. What also stands out is a convincing account of the Miao people. Theirs is a harsh world with strange, sometimes brutal rituals. It also has its own beauty. *Something Like A House* is a moving and inspiring account of a people and a way of life which, against difficult odds, manages somehow to continue'

John Burnside, *Scotsman*

'Smith's narrative is beautifully spare and lean without a trace of sententiousness; his unemotional tone contrasts poignantly with the sometimes lurid and horrific events that engulf Fraser and the villagers'

Malcolm Reid, *Time Out*

'Written with the simple precision of a fable, this novel presents a convincing picture of an alien world. The peasant life of routine filth, leaking roofs and bad-tempered water buffalo is beautifully evoked as Smith turns from a discussion of soil erosion to the finer points of Confucian thought'

Dan Linstead, *Sunday Express*

'Smith is a master of imagery, but his prose also has a precision that renders the most sinister realities all the more stringent'

Rachel Campbell-Johnston, *The Times*

'Smith is a mercurial stylist, his prose confounding and comforting, earth-bound and star-gazing'

Charlie Hill, *Independent on Sunday*

'Smith's lean and inexplicit style lends a dreamlike dislocation and calmness. He has written something far more sensitive than the sensationalist thriller he could have produced, and treats China with complexity and subtlety. A literary event'

Phil Baker, *Sunday Times*

'Beautifully written and utterly gripping, this is an enthralling unfolding of some of China's deepest secrets. It is the only novel on the reading list for my students'

Frank Dikotter, Director, Contemporary China Institute, School of Oriental and African Studies

'It held me gripped from beginning to end. Written with a marvellous spare economy, it miraculously conceals the research that has gone into it . . . the mark of a real storyteller. I am lost in wonder, awe and admiration'

Anthony Howard, political columnist

'If Candide had gone to China and seen horrors, not marvels, this is the story he might have told'

Donna Leon

'It is hard to imagine a more powerful portrayal of peasant life, and of the heroism of those who endure it. Awe-inspiring'

James Roberts,
foreign news editor, *Independent on Sunday*

'The story of a Westerner surviving amid cannibalism and poverty in deepest China, *Something Like a House* is convincing both as a murder mystery and as a portrait of an extraordinary culture'

John Gittings,
South-East Asia correspondent, *Guardian*

'The novel is almost perfectly constructed, though to explain its structural appeal I would have to spill its secrets. Smith has a compressive imagination, able to abbreviate a landscape to a brace of images, or an image to a single word. An old cap left on a hook has grown within itself a "green wig" of mould; a Chinese woman totters by on bound feet "the size of fists".'

Robert MacFarlane, *Observer*

SID SMITH spent the first seven years of his working life in labouring jobs – including woodsman, hod-carrier, railway labourer, gravedigger, stagehand and self-employed gardener. Smith has worked extensively for newspapers and magazines and is now a freelance sub-editor on national newspapers. His second novel, *A House by the River*, is also set in China: an extract is included with this book.

Something Like a House has been shortlisted for the 2001 Whitbread First Novel Award.

SID SMITH

Something Like A House

PICADOR

First published 2001 by Picador

This corrected edition published 2002 by Picador
an imprint of Pan Macmillan Ltd
Pan Macmillan, 20 New Wharf Road, London N1 9RR
Basingstoke and Oxford
Associated companies throughout the world
www.panmacmillan.com

ISBN 0 330 48087 1

Copyright © Sid Smith 2001

The right of Sid Smith to be identified as the
author of this work has been asserted by him in accordance
with the Copyright, Designs and Patents Act 1988.

1 3 5 7 9 8 6 4 2

A CIP catalogue record for this book is available from
the British Library.

Typeset by SetSystems Ltd, Saffron Walden, Essex
Printed and bound in Great Britain by
Mackays of Chatham plc, Chatham, Kent

TO MY MOTHER

What is history? History is nothing but
the development and strife of human races

Liang Qichao

China: a civilization pretending to be a state

Lucian Pye, Massachusetts Institute of Technology

1

He was the only round-eye on board, but nobody noticed. Hugging his ankles like a peasant, he sat alone on the dented metal deck. He avoided faces, as always, watching the river from behind the funnel, quiet in the diesel stink where no one else would come.

First the concrete dock slipped away, then the steep valley sides came close, squeezing the great river. It began to grumble, hurrying them more swiftly out of the mountains. Flat-footed as a Chinaman, he sat on the good canvas rucksack that always reminded him of years before, when he'd been the only round-eye in the Red Guards.

The Guards had wanted to kill him, then disagreed. So they delayed their choice, marching away with the white man who walked like a peasant. On the second day they saw an old man in a field by the road. They poured down into the field and separated into three groups – the swordfish, the dragon and the swallow – competing for who could dig the deepest. Soon the old man was sinking to his knees as the leader slapped his face. They didn't finish their digging. Where they had worked, the soil was buried under gritty subsoil, the field ruined for a thousand years.

Then he was sent to a Red Guard indoctrination camp. He met an old artilleryman who talked about his time firing ten shells a day across the Taiwan Straits. The

Guards had chalked anti-capitalist slogans on the shells, but wrote them on the shell-cases so that the insults were spat at their feet. They had white-washed the murals in local temples and inoculated whole villages in an afternoon, their needles growing blunt on hundreds of arms and spreading dog-tick fever.

His rucksack came from a dead peasant. The Guards had changed a shrine into a pigsty, and then discovered that this was a countryside without pigs. With joyful revolutionary songs they dragged a sow from the rail-head. Six weeks later they returned to the village. There was a ham in the storehouse roof and pig bones hidden under straw, ready to be burned for fertilizer. That afternoon, resting on a hillside, he had watched the executions across the valley. He knew that in the hills there were no scraps for pigs: pigs were a rich man's beast. But the peasants had only said 'Please, please,' as they were led away. He saw the men falling in silence and then the sound like doors closing.

Now he stood up, watching the other passengers from under his cap. He felt trapped again: sometimes there were police on the river boats. He went ashore at the next town and found it crowded with Westerners. They argued in front of tourist hotels, watched from cafes, loitered by racks of postcards – the first whites he had seen in thirty-five years.

'Not like the brochures,' someone said in English. It was a grey-haired man, about his own age, talking to a large woman in a floral dress.

'The ancient marvels of an ageless civilization,' said the woman.

'And toilets to go with it.'

They drifted away as he watched from a doorway. He was thinking how the Chinese had kept him in a secret valley, and how the child he loved had been killed and her bones stolen. He was whispering to their retreating backs.

'My name is Jim,' he murmured, as they vanished round a corner. 'Jim Fraser. Hello. Call me Jim. *I have seen amazing things.*'

2

Fraser was eighteen when he came East. The troopship had docked first at Hong Kong, and he had trailed through the crowds with louder young men who somehow knew their way around.

He pulled his cap low over one eye, though not so low as some of the others. Occasionally he spat. They took a rickshaw ride. Someone got tattooed.

Then they were in a bar near the dockyard, and he was talking to a Chinese woman. Or rather, she talked to him. She wasn't pretty, but he was fascinated because she took care of everything. He didn't need to talk or be nice, he only had to keep his elbow in this puddle on the bar. The beers came, other girls came and went, but the woman kept her hand on his arm and said things which needed no reply.

She took his hand and he felt a great jolt of desire. He looked around the bar, which was suddenly crowded and bright, but his friends from the regiment had left. 'Gone,' said Fraser. 'All gone.'

He wasn't sure if this meant he was abandoned or free, but the woman led him outside, her strong bones gripping through the push of people. 'Very sorry,' he said. 'Very drunk.'

Next they were in a ferry boat. He told the woman that he only felt ill because of the smell of the engine: he was never, never seasick. They travelled for a long time, then climbed a wooden ladder to the shore and passed up an alley in great darkness.

Fraser started to complain, but wasn't displeased. 'I'm going home with a prostitute,' he thought.

Then he was sitting in a tiny room, an old woman watching him. This lasted for some time, but Fraser was glad because when the younger woman came back he had decided what was right. He gave her all his money, even the money in his sock, and said, 'Sleep. Sleep now.'

He woke in utter darkness, knowing what he would do. It was his first time. The woman grumbled and sighed as he entered her, but how effortlessly he was accommodated. China, he thought, China.

When he woke next morning the woman had gone. He went into the tiny room next door and her mother or aunt or madam brought him tea. There seemed no pressure to leave, and anyway he wanted to ask for his money, or at least a part of it. The old woman bustled in and out while Fraser drank the whole sour pot of tea, but it was always impossible. At last, when she was gone for a moment, he hurried down a staircase as narrow as a ladder.

When he got outside he needed to relieve himself. He looked along the tiny street for a bar, but recognized nothing. He stepped a few yards, searching for a quiet alley, but everywhere was crowded with Chinese. Washing spanned the streets, market stalls blocked the way. There was nothing familiar except an anonymous span of sky.

He bundled his army jacket and hid it under his arm. He toiled up and around the tiny alleys while his urgent need came and went and came back stronger than ever. He brushed through crowds, for the first time in his life seeing no one taller than himself. Then he had a brainwave.

He headed quickly downhill. He thought he passed the prostitute's house but wasn't sure and didn't stop. Soon he would find the port. The alley grew suddenly steeper, turned sharply right, and then Fraser halted. In front of him it reared steeply uphill again.

He was standing on stones as big as suitcases. Between them was the glint of water. It was a tiny flat bridge over a tiny stream. He had been descending into a steep valley, and now the street invited him up the other side.

He stepped off the bridge. There was a path running downstream, and he hurried past the backs of wooden houses that grew more squalid. An old man with no teeth quacked from the far bank. Pot-bellied children, naked but for a ragged shirt, paused in their scampering. And still there was nowhere to piss.

Across the stream the houses gave way to a scrubby wood. He teetered across on wobbling stones, but found that the ground between the bushes was trodden solid. He imagined his piss running for yards across the bare earth, and pushed uphill into deeper undergrowth. At last, trembling and sweating, he drained his pee and his strength.

He leaned back against a tree. After a minute he opened his eyes and blinked with surprise. Over the shoulder of a hill he could see the main Hong Kong harbour, crowded with ships. He'd come completely the wrong way.

After a while he climbed further up the wooded slope. At the top he was disappointed again: he had thought Hong Kong was small. Inland, blue hills stepped into the distance, but there was nothing that looked like China.

Then he was shipped to the war.

'Hand grenades have these little squares on them,' the sergeant had said. 'It's like they make bars of chocolate, so that every bugger gets a bit.'

Fraser saw the flash of his grenade that night in Korea. He forgot to duck and a pine tree lit up for a moment like a green army tent. Surely they would ignore him, the Chinese, if they overran the camp. All through the freezing night he was scared and incredulous: whatever he did the Communists would notice even him.

But nobody was killed, just a Chinese, and they tramped through the snow to search the body. It was frozen solid, with bits of blood in its clothes like stained glass, but they raised it with enormous effort and left it sitting on a tree stump, one eye open and a hand cupped by its ear like someone deaf.

They evacuated the camp, part of the general UN collapse, and fled south through the terrible Chinese ambush around Kunu-ri and on to a great Allied regrouping. The ice turned to mud, the rivers flooded and everyone thought they were going home.

Instead a dozen of them climbed into Bren carriers and went back to the war, or 'back to front' as they all said. Two units, one American and one Turkish, had been left behind in the universal rout. They were never found. At least, not before Fraser deserted.

They were parked close to an empty village. The Chinese were coming, and the officer smoked hard as he studied their route back. Fraser was no longer the youngest, but still had to clean the sergeant's boots. He had to lend money, too, which somehow he could never ask for, and before every meal he was sent with a jerrycan to the nearest stream, because there were reports of wells being poisoned.

Here it meant a long hike across a ploughed field. They had been issued with woollen cap-comforters against the bitter winds, but the sergeant insisted they wore them straight, which left their ears exposed: Fraser pulled his cap right down the moment he entered the woods where the Chinese had camped.

There were cigarette packets, a latrine stink, and what looked like a Chinese army newspaper. Its flimsy pages were melting to paste, but Fraser had a favourite picture. An ant raced across the page as he gazed at the broad face of a peasant girl, leaning on a shovel and gazing into the sun. This is what they're fighting for, he thought.

He remembered a story that one of the veterans had told him. It had happened to a friend who was driving a tank in North Africa. Their CO was a bastard. He gave every crew a tarpaulin and made them paint the outline of all the tools they carried. On inspections they laid out this tarpaulin with each tool in its outline, and they'd twice had their pay docked for losing things.

Then the tank was on patrol and shed one of its

tracks. This always took hours to fix, especially on sand, and when they got back they'd be nailed for not keeping it tensioned. They were packing up when they realized they'd lost a brass key the size of a thumb. They searched everywhere, blaming each other, but of course it was sunk somewhere under the sand. They couldn't waste any more time so they set fire to the tank and walked back. It was only four or five miles, and quite pleasant in the evening cool. They had time to sort out a story about running over some kind of mine or unexploded shell.

Fraser tried to pick up the Chinese newspaper, but it fell to bits in his fingers. He threw the jerrycan into the bushes and walked into the woods, directly away from his unit.

He spent two nights amongst ravenous fleas in the deserted village and two days lying flat in the middle of the ploughed field, watching the road. It was very cold, but he thought about the sergeant and the officer trying to explain his desertion. They'd have to admit ill-treating him. They'd be court-martialled.

At last the Chinese came. He wouldn't surrender to front-line troops, waiting instead for cooks and wagon drivers. Then a jeep pulled up. The driver unloaded camp stools, and two officers climbed out and sat drinking tea, a map on the ground between them.

Fraser stood up. He raised his hands and waited for a long minute until the officers grew still.

For three days he sat only on the floor: in guard rooms, outside in the cold, and wedged between the benches on a troop train. Then he was ill. He remembered being picked up by two soldiers and soiling himself and them. For a time he lay in a hospital tent that was crowded but silent.

He was getting better when they put him in an ambulance. He bounced over rough roads, guarded by a soldier in an antiseptic mask. Twice the ambulance stopped and his chamber pot was carried to the roadside. Fraser watched from the window as diesel was poured in and set alight.

At a large prison they took his army clothes and dressed him in thin cotton. He shivered for a week while a sneering young man wrote down everything he said about Korea. After that there was a kind of progress.

He rode a train for four days until it was warm like Hong Kong. In police vans or converted buses he followed a river upstream as the roads got worse and the air cooler. It was obvious when he reached the end of his journey.

3

Very faint and dizzy he had stared without interest at yet another small town. Here, though, he had to get down from the police van. He tottered up steep alleys past dirty wooden houses. Every vista ended with a hill or the river. On the far bank, mountains crowded to the waterside.

He lay down in a locked cell and slept. Twice a day a man in uniform brought his food. Sometimes a young woman opened the iron door and stared at him. She was skinny and small, a kind he liked, though he couldn't understand the red scars on her cheeks.

He tried meeting her eyes, but she watched him coldly, holding her cigarette like a dart. Perhaps she knew that he daren't go home: he had deserted in the face of the enemy and might be shot. For the first time he was worried about China.

He stayed at the clinic for a month. At first he was questioned endlessly about Korea. Watched by the woman, orderlies took blood smears or samples from his chamber pot. Then everyone grew bored. His police guard disappeared and he was moved from his cell. He ate in the small canteen and slept restlessly in a ward of empty beds.

He sat for hours in the day room, ignored by staff who had treated him ten minutes earlier, staring into the clinic's buffalo field. Sometimes a peasant worked there, very quick and lean. He would bow extravagantly to the staff in the day room, sweeping off his cap for extra emphasis.

A smiling man arrived. He had lived in Hong Kong and now taught English to Party workers in the town, but he couldn't understand Fraser. He would ask him to pronounce rare words, to explain situations in Shakespeare, to distinguish *should* from *ought*. He started discussions about colonialism or market economics until they were both embarrassed. Then he fell silent, shredding a cigarette into a curly English pipe clamped in the middle of his desperate grin.

After two or three visits he declared with a sad smile that Fraser had a 'regional dialect', and was therefore 'not greatly useful to an academic such as I'.

Fraser had nowhere to sit but the ward and the day room, nowhere to walk but the corridor between, with its rooms full of filing cabinets or rats in cages. He stared through windows at other buildings that seemed part of the clinic. They were derelict, with scorch marks above the windows and all the glass broken: there were bullet holes in every wall.

He couldn't leave the clinic, he was sure, but the buffalo field seemed less off limits. One afternoon, when the day room was empty, he opened a warping door and stepped into the spring air. The day was lovely, but given an edge by a cold wind from the river. The shadows of clouds raced across the field and up the steep ridge beyond.

The gardener or stockman was spreading forage for the buffaloes. He saw Fraser and was transfixed. He dropped the hay and trotted over, his eyes and mouth wide. He came quite close, his head thrust forward, chattering softly to himself.

He held Fraser's cuff, rubbed a button on his jacket, walked around him, still talking, and at last stared him up and down and asked loud questions in a voice that was half offended. Fraser noticed something that became familiar. It was the earth smell of a healthy peasant, dusty as geraniums.

Whenever the stockman came Fraser brought tea from the canteen. In return he was shown things – when to feed the buffaloes, where to carry the great sacks of food for the caged rats, and how to clear winter trash from the gutters while his new friend held the ladder. The man touched himself on the nose and said his name: Tao Yumi.

Then they had a visitor. She came to the barbed-wire fence round the buffalo field, bright as a parrot in a sky-blue waistcoat, purple turban and black cotton trousers cut to mid-calf. Brilliant embroidered straps criss-crossed her linen blouse.

Perhaps she had been selling things in the town, because she carried two empty baskets on a shoulder pole. She gave Tao a steamed bun, leaning through the barbed wire fence but staring always at Fraser.

Only a young policeman came with them, his collar like a hoop around his skinny neck. Tao and his wife led them through the back door of the clinic and across the stony buffalo field. They ducked under a barbed-wire fence and crossed a narrow strip of bushes.

Beyond was the steep ridge where the policeman lagged behind, pressing on his knees as they climbed. The Taos took Fraser's arm and pointed at things. They made him repeat words and then laughed.

They reached the top of the ridge, but only Fraser looked back at the town. He was worried. The hills were cold, and the Taos too happy.

They walked in single file across the narrow summit. First the clinic disappeared, then the town, then the river, until they saw nothing but the tops of other hills. In the distance were mountains, still capped with snow.

The ridge was a rubble of white stones, with cushions of tough grass behind the larger boulders. Then the valley of the Miao people opened below.

It was a dreadful battlefield, he thought, covered with flooded shellholes. Then he saw they were fields, with buffaloes and people in the grey water.

They followed a zigzag track down the side of the ridge. Next to the track were curved banks holding pools of water. At the bottom they stepped out onto a narrow path between the flooded fields. It soon climbed a low embankment to a cart track, which ran left and right up the middle of the valley. Fraser looked ahead to a village of wooden houses.

It was market day. The policeman had never seen a Miao market, and laughed at the stalls of ragged old clothes, or single razor blades, or slabs of pig fat.

Everyone stared at Fraser. A circle of women, all in purple turbans like Madame Tao, fell silent. A man stood open-mouthed as they stepped over bamboo baskets like a row of torpedoes, each with a little black pig lying helpless. An old woman bent from the waist in amazement, her one silver earring like a shark hook. There was a shout of laughter: someone had recognized the Taos.

More waiting. Fraser squatted outside the biggest house while the policeman went inside. Tao was called, emerging with a grin. Fraser's life was being settled.

They went even further up the valley. A line of women was planting rice in the icy water. They passed a haystack built around a wooden stake. At last the Taos stopped and pointed. Ahead was a little raised island in the fields of water, where half a dozen houses cramped together.

The track narrowed to a footpath. There was a pile of stones, an abandoned plough, and the potent smell of shit. People were waiting in the village yard. A stocky young man stood scowling, hands on hips.

More people came from the houses, chopsticks busy while their eyes widened over the rim of their bowls. All the women wore purple turbans. Firewood leaned to dry against every wall. A midden, tall as a man, stood and stank between the houses.

There was a terrifying little boy. He stood apart from the rest, barefoot and thin. His hair was a helmet of dirt. His clothes were grey sacking, hanging in rags to his bony knees. Perhaps he had risen from the grave to greet them.

Fraser seemed to faint or half-faint. He was helped inside to a stool at a cluttered table. Villagers pressed close as he swayed over a steaming cup, and at last he was put to bed. The bed was lumpy but warm under a grey quilt, and he slept and slept.

He was on a ledge behind a curtain, and dozed through the days listening to Madame Tao in the main room. In the evenings Tao arrived from the fields and the couple woke him with rice.

At night he lay awake as the wind rushed between the houses. He was troubled by the calling of children and woke once to a chicken's beady gaze. People lifted the curtain while he dozed.

'You were young,' Madame Tao said later. 'Very young and small, so nobody hated you.'

On the third evening Fraser sat up in bed. He peered around the curtain and the Taos rose with welcoming cries. Madame Tao gave them each a cup and poured hot water from a blackened pot. Fraser, because he was ill, got a pinch of tea. He sat up, shy in his alcove, while the Taos fussed around him.

This was the start of his new life.

4

He got to know the house first. It was half-timbered like something in a book, but very grey. There was only one room. The floor was hard dirt, no different from the village yard: in the centre was a fire-pit where a cooking pot crouched on three stones. Wood smoke lay in skeins at head height, filtering slowly out through the thatched roof.

There was a battered table, some low stools, and a sagging bed in the corner which the Taos screened each night with a blanket. Most things were kept in sacks, which stood against the walls or hung from nails. Rusty hooks held a couple of farm tools. A stool was taken from the wall and passed to him with ironic ceremony.

Madame Tao's bright clothes lay in a box next to the bed, and she took rice or water or maize from three hip-high earthenware pots, padded with sacking, which stood behind the table.

The table was the centre, and Fraser didn't yet feel he could share it. Tao Yumi sat in the middle of one side, and ranged around him were his pipe, tobacco, knife, plate and oil lamp. All evening, with humour and insight, he lectured Fraser in a language he couldn't understand. He sharpened the knife on a slip of stone, spitting on the work and exercising great care as to the angle of the grind.

He wiped the knife on his trousers and passed it to

Fraser with many encouraging comments: Fraser understood that the knife was magnificently sharp, yet not so sharp that the edge would burr.

After a few nights, like the people at the clinic, Tao grew bored. He confined his comments to Madame Tao, who sat at the table end in the outer limit of the lamplight, bent to her embroidery or basket-making. She hardly spoke, except to chuckle with her husband or agree with his insights. Tao laid his whole forearms on the table, but she only touched it with her hands.

Fraser sat on his stool and looked into the dim roof space under the thatch, which was full of cobwebs, dark packages, and things drying in the wood smoke – great bundles of maize cobs and little bushes that must be herbs. He had missed his chance to sit at the table. The maize hung from the bamboo rafters on ropes which passed through wooden discs: there must be rats, he knew, because he had seen such discs on the mooring ropes for the troopship.

When he could wait no longer he hurried through the back door to the village latrine. It was a patch of ground in one corner of the little island, with a waist-high wall overlooked by half the houses. Fraser crouched down even to pee, squatting astride two planks laid over a stinking pit. He could see how the planks were moved as the pits filled, because all around were sunken patches covered with earth and wood ash.

He was given maize to husk, and a cheap knife which couldn't keep an edge and bent like tin. After two or three days he took his stool to the front door. It had a high wooden threshold like on a ship, and he sat behind it in the gloom and watched.

He had seen a farm in Scotland, and understood the red hands of the villagers, their layers of shapeless clothes, the doors open to the cold all day. But these people made new sounds when they stumbled, or sat down after a long day, or called across the fields – when there were different calls for men and women.

Other things became clear. The midden was near so that no one could steal from it, and the little boy wore terrifying rags because his father stayed in the village all day, smoking and staring over the fields and doing no work.

Everything was made of earth or fraying wood, with the metal tools guarded like bullion. When he dreamed, he was in the floating, floorless space below the thatch, with dark bundles all around and the Taos in the lit room below.

His first friend was a buffalo. It lived in the head-man's house in a room cobbled with river stones. When no one was looking he slipped in from the yard, pushing open the half-door and squatting in the gloom until the beast stopped its nervous sighs to lick the salty skin between his fingers.

He traced its nose-rope from the knot behind its ears, under the eyes with their girlish lashes, along the soft muzzle, and into and through the great damp nostrils. Its horns were hard as wood. Without being told he shovelled its droppings to the midden.

He now had a route into the Taos' house, turning left

directly inside the door then sitting on a stool against the wall. Or he sat on the edge of his alcove: whenever he liked he could fall back onto his bed, the curtain closing behind him. Under the cotton mattress was a wooden beam. It was marked with rings where, until he arrived, the earthenware jars had been kept from the damp floor.

Madame Tao showed him the springs. They were half a mile away, where the valley narrowed to a rocky cleft. Along the foot of a little cliff were beds of gravel, wet with a water seep. The biggest upsurging was in a pool the size of a sink. It was choked with weeds, but in the middle was a bulge of water like a face.

Every day he waited until the women had taken their turns with the village buckets, and then slipped quickly out of the house. Sometimes the ragged boy watched him totter away along the narrow path above the fields.

The buckets were wooden like little barrels, with square wooden handles like a bit from a ladder. Even empty they bent the shoulder pole. Fraser didn't yet understand the tripping steps of the villagers, who used the flexing pole to help their progress, and he often stopped to rest, trying to grasp this new place.

The valley was two or three hundred yards wide, every inch covered with fields of water and the spidery raised paths between them. There were only two trees, planted for shade in Market Village half a mile down the valley. Flooded fields climbed the valley sides, smaller and smaller plots behind stony banks, with little streams trickling through.

The headman's wife had beautiful buckets of galvanized steel. Her husband was the stocky young man who had scowled when Fraser first arrived. They lived with two babies in the only house with an upper floor: attached to the back was a second kitchen, with three waist-high walls and a straw roof, so that the cooking fire wouldn't warm the house during the summer. The headman continued to scowl.

Fraser could tick off the other families: the Taos; the ragged boy and his parents; and a strange couple who lived beyond the headman's house and didn't matter. Two houses were empty, used for stores and tools.

Now Fraser only noticed the stink of shit occasionally, as if it came on a breeze. He was no longer startled when the multicoloured women emerged from houses like farm sheds.

One morning the buffalo was gone. Madame Tao laughed behind her fist as Fraser came from its byre. All day, crouched on his stool, he watched the villagers in the fields, jealous of their time with the buffalo. A great scoop was gone from the midden.

In the evening the buffalo came back with the villagers. Like them it was spattered with mud. Even the ragged boy's father had been working, his jacket torn where the headman had beaten him again. Tao hung his mattock on the wall and couldn't speak.

Next morning Fraser was woken early. The buffalo was waiting in the village yard, and Tao placed Fraser's hand on its nose-rope. The men grinned and pointed at the beast, saying, 'Miu.' Was this the creature's name or the word for buffalo? Either way it was like 'moo' and easy to remember. When he said it everyone laughed, but it was the first word he learned.

The buffalo's spit ran over his fist as he led it down the narrow causeway, dragging manure on a kind of stretcher or sledge. They had nothing else to do all day. The buffalo, its nose-rope hobbled to a foreleg, wandered along the main path nibbling the new grass, and Fraser followed its mincing back legs, tapping it away from the edges with a stick and feeding it tasty morsels of spring growth.

Everything was strange. There were no wheelbarrows, only stretchers that two men would carry or one would pull. Instead of rucksacks they wore long baskets. They carried manure in baskets on shoulder poles. Two women stood in the cold water, levelling the mud with a single shovel, one pulling a rope tied near the blade. Tao had an axe like a dinner plate.

After a week his holiday was over. Every day he left his army boots on the bank and slithered into the cold water, scooping out mud with his hands to mend the earth banks where they had slid into the fields during the winter. But he watched the buffalo.

Tao had an unexpected celebrity. He walked behind the beast, twisting and lifting a great wooden plough through the mud. He flicked a leather rein and talked to the creature with short cries. Everyone could see that the round-eye wanted to help, but Tao ignored him.

That summer Tao was sacked from the clinic. He had been hired by a young official who was still stirred by Communist principles, noting with approval a poster on the wall of the Party offices. It proclaimed, 'Cooperation between the Chinese and the minority tribes will make the nation strong'. But he knew that the Chinese were everywhere dominant.

Throughout the country, wherever the valleys were wide and the plains fertile, the Chinese worked fields that raised two and three harvests a year. But the fields of the minority tribes were squeezed into rocky valleys or leaned against hills until the thin soil slid away.

The official was ashamed of these ancient wrongs. He began reading about the Miao, the most numerous of local tribes, who said that even the rain was a tax agent because it took their land and washed it to the Chinese — who they still called 'the Invader'.

Tao seemed the perfect employee, so happy and eager, doffing his cap to the day room windows, saluting technicians and the visiting Party officials with their pretty secretaries. The fatter the official and the prettier his consort the more sprightly he grew, nodding and laughing through the glass.

Typical Miao stuff, thought Madame Fei. She had recently been confirmed as director of the clinic, and at once discovered that she couldn't bear to eat with her foolish husband. For a few weeks she took tea in the day room, where Tao's antics became irritating.

She couldn't dismiss a man for laughing, even though his laughter said that being a Party official with a beautiful companion was nothing much, since even a Miao with bad teeth could be happy. Instead she decreed that, now the grass was growing again, there was insufficient work for a stockman.

She delegated Tao's dismissal to the same young

idealist who had hired him and had negotiated his acquisition of the round-eye Fraser. Tao nodded at the man's explanation, but knew that he was once again punished for being a Miao.

The young idealist was himself soon dismissed, so there was no one to listen to Fraser when he sneaked to the clinic a few weeks later. Embarrassed and desperate, he wandered the corridors in his filthy clothes, looking for someone to talk to. He wanted to explain that the village was impossible, that he had to be moved. But he was standing alone in the day room when the police arrived.

Madame Fei watched him being escorted back up the ridge behind the clinic, so angry that the red smallpox scars pulsed in her cheeks. She would write to the ministry again: the round-eye should be back in his cell at the clinic, until she was ready to begin her work.

Next year the ragged boy's father left. His wife moped about the village or came to the Taos to cry, and the child watched all day down the empty track. Fraser thought that the boy was perhaps related to the Taos: perhaps the villagers were all related.

The woman's name was Joy, as near as he could say it. In the hot afternoons, while the crop ripened and there was nothing to do, she brought her stool to the Taos and talked hopelessly while the boy stood at her knee, twisting in her apron.

Eventually, Tao would stamp outside with a growl while his wife sighed and leant back, relighting the twist of cheap tobacco which stood upright in her pipe like a cigar. Then Joy would turn without a pause to Fraser, who understood nothing, not even her need to blankly complain. Her only amusement was making him say her name.

Nothing was heard of Joy's husband until the following spring, but then she came to the house again. She showed them a letter which she had taken to the town to be read. She passed the letter to Fraser, pointing at the boy and saying, 'Father.' Her bare feet were brown under the stool, her dirty toes gripping and twisting together for comfort. She had white teeth. Her eyes were puffy slits like a boxer's.

As usual, Fraser was obsessed with the ploughing. He was bringing rice seedlings from the nursery fields, but between trips he crouched on the paths to watch.

The buffalo hated these fields, he knew. Its eyes rolled because its sides were unprotected: it was in open ground, with no herd for company. Nor would Fraser stand where Tao stood, on the animal's rear flank, where it could neither see nor kick.

Tao pulled on the nose-rope to turn the beast, slapping its haunch when at last the great shoulders pointed in the right direction. Fraser felt in his ankles how he would do it. It would be like rowing a heavy boat through waves: never trying to stop it, but helping when it bobbed the right way.

Under his breath he practised the liquid whistling which Tao used for imitating the sound of running water: it was for late summer, when the animal was too hot and tired to piss and there was no water in the fields to splash its genitals.

But Fraser could only touch the buffalo twice a day. He went quickly to the byre in the morning, wondering if the beast would want to work, then led it to the stretcher. He waited all day until the creature hauled itself onto the main path, its back legs knotting like the legs of a strong old man, muddy water streaming from its belly. Tao would turn away, dropping the rope into Fraser's hands and striding ahead while the round-eye led the beast back to its home.

One evening Joy caught up with them. The two men said nothing as she chattered. The nights were still cold, and her words turned white in the air.

She fell silent when they reached the village, then she seemed almost angry. She was talking to both of them but pushing Fraser in the chest, her brown fingers very strong.

She dashed to her house, which was opposite the Taos', and pulled a stool from the doorway. She must have planned this. She took Fraser's sleeve and led him to the stool, and he sat embarrassed outside her door. Tao watched, then went into his house.

Joy grew calm. She brought Fraser a cup of rice water and sat beside him on her threshold. Villagers emerged and disappeared, but it was cold and doors were closing against the dusk. Madame Tao came to her door, then vanished.

Why shouldn't I sit here? thought Fraser. He would sit here, he decided, and drink water with this solitary woman.

He waited under the gaze of her solemn little boy until she called them in. It was dark in the house. It made him think of the Taos, who argued every night about the oil lamp. Madame Tao muttered as she tried to cook in the half dark, but Tao waited so long to light the lamp that often he had to hunt it through the room with a lit match.

There was no lamp here. They ate dumplings and rice by the feeble light of the firepit. No firewood leaned against her house and Joy burned only rice straw and old maize cobs.

It was draughty, too. The villagers used sheets of paper in their windows instead of glass, but there had been no new paper in Joy's house for many winters. She seemed to notice that Fraser was cold, because she went outside and returned with an armful of logs, stolen perhaps from the Taos.

She and the boy sat whispering in a quilt, but Fraser thought about the earth floor in Miao houses. It made you see how a house was only a box set in a field, even the kind of house he had dreamed about in the orphanage. He had been no older than the little boy. He had grown up hoping for quietness, and a fire in the evening.

The Taos were in bed when he got back. He took off his boots and jacket and lay awake under the quilt. He remembered Madame Tao fitting new window paper. He knew the trick of it – the glue made with boiled rice, and how you rubbed the paper with lamp oil to keep out the rain. He thought about buying firewood and a lamp for Joy. He could sell his army boots.

Next day, while he rested in the fields with the men, Joy came across from the women and gave him a sweet dumpling. He didn't see who laughed, only that it wasn't

Tao. In the evening she loitered behind as they walked back along the narrow paths. She was singing her songs and playing with the little boy. Because of this Fraser was the first to see what had happened.

Joy's cups and plates were scattered across the village yard. He stared, trying to understand, but Joy pushed past him. She was transformed. Barefoot among the broken pots, she screamed at the villagers, throwing bits of crockery. But despite her anger she was crying. Somebody shouted back, but the argument was won and people were drifting away.

Tao went indoors. There were raised voices, and Fraser's stool flew out and the door slammed shut. Weeping, Joy carried the silent little boy into her house.

Fraser lifted his stool from the broken pots. Only the headman watched as he stood alone in the yard. But it was cold and getting dark. He carried his stool indoors, back to the Taos.

5

'Food,' said Fraser. 'Buffalo.'

Tao nodded, and Fraser led the beast to its room in the headman's house. The harvest was in, and the women were feeding rice sheaves through the threshing box, cranking it like a barrel organ.

Joy was drunk with the men. For two days they had celebrated with the buffalo, leading it around the village and then out to the boundaries of their fields.

Here they had met the men from Market Village, and planted flags on the cairn at their mutual border. Everyone was drunk, and the buffalo was decorated with flowers, chicken blood, and rope made of twisted rice stalks. There was no cordiality: Market Village had four buffaloes, and the biggest had horns tipped with brass sheaths.

It was their smallest buffalo which emptied its bowels. The excrement spattered into the silence, and a man from Market Village skipped aside to save his new canvas shoes.

Fraser was standing well back, because he felt himself an outsider. He had just realized the problem of the droppings, that here was a foreign buffalo shitting on their side of the boundary, when Tao jumped forward. He scooped the hot droppings from the ground and caught them as they fell. Everyone watched in silence, even the men from the village, but Tao shouted in triumph as he threw the excrement in wide arcs over the village fields.

Now Fraser sighed. He tethered the buffalo to the wall of the byre and lit the oil lamp. He fed the animal from his hand, its thick lips fumbling after the maize like a boxer picking up pennies. Its tongue was rough. Its breath smelled of grass and old cheese, sour as a nursing mother.

His love frightened the beast and a rare light came to its eyes, far down like water in a well. He put his cheek to the deep boat of its ribs. He stroked the corded front legs, ropes that could hold a ship, searching for ticks. Its horns were perfect sickles, curving back over its neck. If it lived long enough, would the points meet?

Fraser snuffed out the lamp. His legs were blistered again: he had been carrying shit from the latrine to the fields, and the baskets always dripped. He closed his eyes and sat at peace in the dark, his back against the cold wall, his head on the buffalo's side.

He was wondering if Tao would buy him a cap for the winter. All through the fetid summer his old cap had hung on a hook against the wall. He had taken it down against the first chill and found the fabric slimy and a wig of green mould inside.

He woke to low voices. Faint starlight leaked in through the open door, but he didn't know the two men. As he stood up they flinched backwards, then one of them slashed at the buffalo. Fraser only recognized them as they ran out. They were from Market Village. They had been at the cairn.

By then he was struggling with the buffalo. It had leapt away from the hurt, crushing him against the wall. He dragged its head down with the nose-rope, but still it bucked and twisted, braying in pain.

Fraser squirmed free, rolling himself over the animal's back. He ran to the door, searching over the flat fields for the two men. He could see nothing, only Tao hurrying towards the noise.

The buffalo was calm but vicious, aiming its back legs at any approach. Two stripes on its rump bled to the floor. Fraser was shaking with anger. He pointed in the Miao style, fingers pressed together, chopping his hand towards Market Village, but no words came.

On Tao's advice they pissed in a bucket and threw it across the wound. They locked the byre and set off down the valley with Joy's son, now a sturdy eight-year-old who the village called Young Tao. The child was better dressed: Fraser's work points meant extra payments from the commune, so Tao could pass a little money to Joy. The headman, too drunk to intervene, followed complaining through the dark until he slipped down a bank and fell asleep in the mud.

Market Village was well guarded. They had come along the valley side to avoid the open fields, but the Buffalo Festival was a time for village raids. Drunken men staggered about the market square, but others sat quietly in their doorways, and scouts lay among the fields.

They were spotted at once. A shout of alarm turned to laughter. They were already running when stones began to bounce on the track and thud into the muddy fields.

Next day, Tao and Fraser had to pull the thatch from their roof. They piled it in the village yard, and four policemen, angry after their long walk, watched it burn. They threw Tao's mattock and sieve onto the fire. After they had left with Tao, the villagers laughed and pointed at Fraser's forehead. It was smeared with blood from the night before.

The stones had driven them towards the town. Tao was the loudest, as usual, shouting back towards Market Village and laughing angrily with Young Tao. Then they set out, Tao striding ahead, following a stream that curved out of the darkness to join them. Fraser hadn't been this far from the village since he arrived from the clinic. For the first time he understood the valley.

This stream had once flowed direct from the springs above the village. Now it was delayed in paddy fields, hurried through sluices, bewildered into irrigation ditches. Even its little tributaries fed water terraces as they trickled down the valley sides. Only below Market Village, where the land was too stony to farm, could its waters collect themselves again and run uninterrupted into the big river downstream of the Chinese town.

To their left was the Hog, the ridge he had crossed on his way from the clinic and the town. Behind them its rump merged with the main mass of the hills, ahead it dwindled as the valley widened, until its snout disappeared to nothing where it met the river. To their right, the valley side was even steeper, marking the beginning of the serious hills.

They were downstream of Market Village, so it was an easy climb over the Hog. There is no Buffalo Festival among the Chinese, and only a few lights shone in the town below. Fraser had guessed their target.

As they descended, they cut back along the ridge, creeping through the bushes to the buffalo field behind the clinic. They rested against the wooden shed where Tao and Fraser had stacked so many bags of rat food, and Tao crept towards the biggest animal.

It was more nervous than a working buffalo and started to get up. Tao lay on the grass, reaching towards it at full stretch with a handful of boiled rice. The buffalo stayed down.

He stopped feeding the animal, which at once grew restless, perhaps smelling the rice in his pocket. Tao edged to his knees as the buffalo nuzzled his jacket. He dropped a handful of rice on the ground, so that the animal stretched to reach it.

Then he stroked something past its neck. It stood up quickly and shook its head as if shaking off flies. It smelled something and jinked to the side. Its spurting blood made a black web in the air, but the beast felt nothing from the sharp blade.

It stood for a minute, its legs spread for flight, its ears cocked at the hissing of blood on the grass. Then it lost interest. It grew sleepy again. It knelt down clumsily and its nose touched the ground. It gave shuddering snores and rolled over.

Tao stripped naked and opened the buffalo under the small ribs. He dug out the great liver and laid it on his jacket like a baby. He cut off the buffalo's tongue, tail, and silvery white penis and gave them to Fraser. Young Tao snatched the penis, which was a metre long and slack as a dead snake.

They went back over the Hog by the quickest route, where the slope was so steep that they had to scramble up a trickling river of small stones. It was dangerous in the dark, burdened with the exhausted child and the bits of buffalo, and Fraser arrived at the top with a long scrape down his arm. Tao remembered something: he opened his bundle and smeared their faces with blood.

At the house the penis and tail were wrapped in cloth and buried by the firepit. The tail would make low-grade medicines, but Tao knew a secret way of drying the pizzle, which he would use as his own special whip for herding buffalo.

Next morning he called everyone in the village to eat the liver and tongue. It was unfortunate that the Festival was past, but there was still strong medicine in the meat. He gave Fraser some of the tongue, but the liver would be wasted on a Christian. They ate quickly because they could see the police wagon in Market Village.

Tao spent a week in the cells. He admitted nothing and at last was taken into the yard behind the station, where a corporal and a couple of young recruits wrapped rags around their fists, beat him and sent him home.

Old Tao laughed even as they hit him, because the corporal was the same young policeman who had first brought Fraser to the village, and had reappeared next morning, cold and distraught after a night in the hills, because Tao had given him wrong directions.

When Old Tao got home, Fraser and Madame Tao had cleaned the house of the filth shaken from the thatch, which the villagers had replaced. Joy arrived with a glass of Shanghai whisky. There was an understanding that it came from the headman, who was often seen leaving her house.

Perhaps even the dead buffalo was lucky. Sooner or later Madame Fei would have signed an order at the clinic. It would have been shot with anthrax darts, fed cholera serum, or injected with bubonic plague.

6

Joy had left, and Old Tao was convulsed. This changed everything.

Young Tao had no idea where his mother had gone, only that another letter had come from his father. For a few days he ate with the Taos, returning to his old house to sleep. He seemed to like the arrangement, but Old Tao had his eye on Fraser's ledge.

'You go,' he told Fraser that night. He frowned heavily, because he wanted no sentiment. Fraser had served his purpose but now they had an heir. 'Talk to the headman,' said Tao. 'He can find you a place.'

The village still had two empty houses, and Tao fretted at its consequent poverty – one plough, one miserable buffalo, no cart. He nagged at men from Market Village to move with their families, transferring a field or two when they came. He was too much of a showman for this sad isolation at the end of the valley. But neither house should be wasted on a hairy foreigner with no hope of marriage. He too would talk to the headman: Fraser should leave the village.

But next morning the round-eye had gone, taking his quilt and a sackful of rice. Tao wandered half asleep into the village yard. Bewildered, he stared at the old store-house. It had been empty for a decade, but smoke curled lazily from the roof.

It was small and therefore easy to defend. Its stout

front door had real metal hinges, and there were wooden bars on the one window. The roof was tile, patched with old corrugated iron. It takes great effort to squeeze through thatch, but it closes undamaged behind you: a tiled roof is easier, but the tiles drop from their batons like plates from a shelf and the expense is terrible. The storehouse had once been used for valuables, but now held a few old sacks.

Tao went for the headman. If he disapproved then Fraser must leave or face an irritable police squad. But Tao and the headman had recently disagreed.

Tao had decided that the new metalled road beside the river was too dangerous for the buffalo: nothing was worse, he explained, than a split hoof. But if the animal couldn't carry their goods to the town market, said the headman, there was no point keeping it. The creature was only needed in the fields for a few weeks each year, and they could rent one from Market Village at the normal rate: one hour of a buffalo's time for two hours of a man's. This was a good arrangement, considering the cost of feeding an animal all year, just for the sake of Tao's vanity.

Now the headman stared at the wisp of smoke. Fraser was never any trouble. He hardly spoke, and then was scarcely understandable. The headman had hated him at first for the extra worry he brought: even now, half the villagers complained that he ate their food and did no work, and the rest said that he shamed them by working too hard. But it seemed that the young foreigner only wanted to endure and be left alone.

Fraser was no more than a bent back trudging to the

fields, or a stooped shape among the rice. There was no reason why Old Tao should ever have profited from him, the headman thought, nor why the youngster shouldn't have a house, at least until more deserving tenants arrived. In the meantime, he told Tao, he was going back to his fire.

Tao beat his forehead. In theory he could go to the authorities in the town, but they would only refer back to the headman. Beyond that they could have no interest in an old house at the far end of a Miao valley.

Because of the rice, Fraser wouldn't go hungry, but Tao at once wondered about water. Even here he was unlucky. It started to rain, driving him indoors to plot. It wasn't until dusk that he noticed the holes in the storehouse roof.

At some point during the day Fraser had eased the tiles apart in half a dozen places near the eaves. Since then, water had drained in to fill whatever containers were stored inside, including – Tao remembered with rage – a galvanized steel bath: he had used it for his own water until part of the bottom rusted through.

He threw wet handfuls from the midden onto the roof, but knew that no one from a Miao village would care about a little buffalo dung. He wouldn't go so far as to raid the latrine.

He would wait for Fraser to come out, so that the house could somehow be sealed against him. Then he noticed that Young Tao had vanished.

The boy stayed with Fraser for a month. Old Tao scowled from his threshold across the village yard, but there was always one of them at home. Fraser even started improvements with a rusty crowbar he found on a roofbeam.

Old Tao watched bewildered as its tip emerged through the house-side. By the following day there was a narrow window in the south wall, to catch the best of the light. Young Tao laid the crowbar exactly back in its rust stain.

Tao ignored Fraser, but never stinted his characteristic rambling persuasions on Young Tao. He stopped the boy in the fields or the village yard, or came to the house when Fraser was away, trying to peer inside while he outlined the economic importance of repopulation.

He spluttered in frustration at the stubborn little figure in the doorway, but didn't quite dare to brush him aside. The youngster only said that he would move to the Taos' as soon as Fraser was left alone.

Even here Old Tao was out-thought. No sooner had he abandoned the struggle than Young Tao was again sleeping at his mother's house. When Tao complained, the boy ate with Fraser for a week.

It was strange to be alone. He often woke in the dark, as he had years ago in the empty ward at the clinic, and admired his new window. He had cut it at the top of the wall because he didn't know how to fit a lintel. He would find out though, and make a back door.

He slept on a pile of sacks, his shoes and clothes kept close around him. But slowly he filled the house. It was easy to hang his hat on the wall, as he had at the Taos', but it was a special step when he found a nail in the door, right across the room, and hung up his jacket.

He would be poor, like anyone keeping a house alone, but would eventually get state issues of meat, cloth and cooking oil. With many repetitions and much miming, he confirmed with the headman that he would get a little money when the state buyers came for the rice harvest. Not a full share, said the headman, because that wouldn't be fair on Tao Yumi, but perhaps the money that Tao would have given to Joy, plus a little extra for Fraser's year of work in the fields.

The brief winter came, when only the women worked – sewing and making baskets and fussing around the house while their men walked to Market Village to get drunk, or stared into the firepit, or went to bed to drive out the damp in time for night. But Fraser was busy on his vexatious roof, scavenging the valley for rice straw and the useless tough leaves of maize plants, which he could use for thatch. A few witty drops still came through, making slicks of mud on the earth floor.

He cooked his rice in the one sound corner of his tin bath, propped at an angle over the firepit he had dug. It was cold now: mountains on the horizon had caps of snow, and frost sometimes whitened the upper slopes of the valley, though it was gone by noon.

He couldn't afford a store of logs, but each rest day morning he got a little money from the headman, who had the authority to make advances on the harvest payment, especially since Fraser was kind enough to work on his private field. In the afternoon he laboured up from Market Village with a bundle of wood: he got a discount for cutting it himself.

He often saw Young Tao at the market. He would cautiously nod to the strange child and buy him a lump of dog-meat dipped in brine. They stood in silence for a while, watching the barber or the man with a sewing machine, then Young Tao was gone.

The boy ate with the Taos and played around their door, running in and out with a twig he pretended was an aeroplane, but he still slept alone in his mother's house. Sometimes he fell asleep at the Taos' after his evening meal, but they always carried him back across the yard: if he woke at their house he ignored them for days.

It was disturbing to see the child in his empty house: Madame Tao said he was waiting for Joy, and Old Tao talked again about the village and its sad decline. But the boy was only sullen with adults, and Fraser often saw him around the valley with the boys from Market Village.

Young Tao began to range more widely, sometimes attending the school in Market Village or helping Old Tao in the fields, but usually disappearing for the day into the hills or along the river bank. He threw stones at the boats heading upstream to the town, made whistles from the bark of parasol trees, and wove baskets out of rice straw to trap tiny fish among the rocks of the chill river. Sometimes the boys saw a pig on the river road and left their games to follow it to the market, squabbling to hold the basin for its blood, then watching the daylong dismemberment.

Young Tao liked the market almost as much as Fraser. Every week the round-eye spent longer collecting his wood, pretending to consider a purchase among the stalls selling rat-traps, rope, tools and food. By bedtime the wood was gone, having warmed him all evening and cooked his rice for the week.

He spent the rest of his free time in bed, dozing from dusk to dawn, fully dressed, amazed at his vivid memories. He remembered the dormitory in the orphanage and the beatings delivered after dark by the older boys: he had lain with his eyes squeezed shut, hoping to be ignored. Now he was in the middle of China, warm and alone where no one could find him.

He smiled in the dark, thinking about the Taos, who now seemed his friends. Every winter they had argued about sealing the back door, which rattled on its leather hinges. Tao itched with schemes for covering it with sandbags or an old mattress, or packing rags into its draughty gaps. But Madame Tao allowed no chamber pot in the house and therefore no barrier to the village latrine. She wouldn't spend the winter staggering round the house-end in the dark, especially when Tao would no doubt relieve himself on the ground as soon as he was out of earshot. Fraser changed his mind about cutting a back door.

The warmth of his bed roused the lice from his clothes. Madame Tao had always said that village food would make his blood bitter, so the lice would trouble him less. He had never noticed such an effect, but realized that his new house had been empty for years.

He crept out into the dark, wrapped in a sack, and

spread his clothes under the waters of the nearest flooded field. Before dawn, he twisted and beat the clothes, paying special attention to the seams, hoping to crush any lice which hadn't drowned.

He got dressed and found he was clean. If there were no eggs in his bed he would go to the springs as soon as the weather warmed, and take the first bath of his two years in the village.

He could also let his hair grow from the fuzz worn by every man in the valley. Old Tao had always cut Fraser's hair in a ceremony they both hated. Whatever happened with the house, Fraser decided, he would never again submit to that.

He made an oil lamp from a bit of bootlace poked through the side of a tin can, using a strict measure of kerosene until he discovered the inconvenience of letting the lace dry out and scorch. On every trip to the latrine he snatched a handful of straw from Tao's roof, and now the sacks under his bed were full. He wove a mat of straw for a bootscraper, which Tao at once took for his own house.

One rest day he arrived too early at Market Village and walked on down the valley, following the cart track by the stream. He recognized where they had climbed the Hog on the night Old Tao killed the clinic buffalo, but didn't stop.

The valley sides fell back, their steep hills growing humble, and the ground turned to a broad swath of pebbles and tough grass that not even the Miao would cultivate. It was strange to see so much open ground. The stream grew wide and still. Straight ahead, across the river, were colossal scree slopes, the grey water glittering at their feet.

But first came the river road, crossing the mouth of the Miao valley on its way to the town. Occasional wagons roared over the stream on a new concrete bridge, and in the distance a solitary peasant pushed a wheel-barrow.

The bridge had one concrete foot in the shallow water. Fraser grew closer and saw that someone was splashing there in the gloom. It was a Chinese, dragging out the lush green river weeds. He looked up, shocked to see Fraser. He packed up quickly and hurried to the road, water streaming from the long tresses of weeds that hung down his back.

He looked at Fraser again as he hurried towards the town, and called out angrily. Fraser stared back with a scowl: this was the Miao stream and its weeds must go to Miao compost heaps.

He explored under the bridge, then stood by the road to watch the traffic. Black birds like crows were circling a patch of land between the road and the river. Below them was a multicoloured heap. He walked towards it and found the town dump.

He went there every rest day morning before the market. The rarest, greatest prize was pickle jars, which he used as cups or to store food. He found a wine bottle and made a proper village lamp, the wick pushed through a little disk of metal, cut from a tin can. There were lots of these cans, which he washed in the river on the way home. Now he could shave every day.

His whiskers were more and more shaming, so he

hung a tin can over his lamp each evening, and by bedtime the water was warm enough to soften his stubble. Each can lasted a week or two before it burned through. He thought of the monstrous expense of cooking pots.

Fraser stood at ease in his own doorway. He drank rice water and nodded at Wang Dechen, a thoughtful man who lived with his sister in the house next door. Wang was so thoughtful and his sister so secretive that Tao endlessly wondered about their living arrangements, certain they offered no prospect of a proper family.

Tao never listened to Wang, turning away before he could deliver his boring judgements. Madame Tao, meanwhile, judged a household by how far up the valley it drew its water. Wang dipped his bucket into the first water upstream of the village. For much of the year this was a flooded field.

Every time they met, Wang told Fraser a little more about the water. He didn't take it, only borrow it, so the headman was wrong to say he was upsetting the levels around the young rice. He showed Fraser a bit of limestone, which he called *zeb qaub*, and demonstrated how it settled the mud. Otherwise, he said, the water was no different from spring water, except perhaps for a week or two after the fields were fertilized from the latrine.

Fraser decided he would think a little further about Wang's system, and not yet adopt it.

Everything was different, thanks to the house. By spring he had grown to fill it, and opened his door to welcome the warm air. A swallow flashed around the room and out again, thrumming like an arrow. No swallows could nest here now: it was Fraser's house.

One afternoon, when the sun had its foot in his door, he crept around his little room, examining the dusty pages stuck to the mud walls. All the village houses had their selection, torn from magazines or Party newspapers or *The Farmer's Calendar*. Or there were leaflets handed out by the state rice buyers, showing when to drain the fields or how to build a better latrine or midden, good advice which the villagers took pride in ignoring. But these posters were dry as old leaves.

He found a bit of carved wood that might have been broken from expensive furniture. He put it carefully on the windowledge. There was broken glass, too, as if there had been a celebration long ago: with vague dread he saw that one of the fragments bore a familiar label. He wanted to forget everything before China, but here was the name of a Scottish distillery.

Then he found the teeth. They were trodden into the dirt at the bottom of the wall, three of them, very human, still attached to a broken piece of bone, and worn down as if from an old man. He touched his mouth and decided they were an eye-tooth and its two neighbours. He kept the teeth for a while, then left them under a stone near the springs.

The state rice buyer was angry. He sat at his trestle table in Market Village and shouted until his assistants laughed. It was bad enough paying a round-eye: he wouldn't tolerate dealing with the only man in the valley who could sign his name.

Fraser had spent hours learning the Chinese characters from his ration card, but ended up like everyone else – with a chit for payment at the post office in the town, and an enduring red stain where he had pressed his thumbprint in the buyer's ledger.

The summer storms came early, sending women shrieking from the fields as fat drops pounded their straw hats: the men followed with hunched shoulders, cloth caps flattened on their scalp. Melt water arrived from the mountains and for a month the river flooded into the mouth of the Miao valley, swilling under the concrete road bridge and carrying away half the town dump.

One rest day, Fraser climbed the Hog. He wanted to see his house from above. It was very hot, so he paused often on the steep track between the terraces.

In the rain and heat the valley was flourishing. Rice plants thickened in the terraces around him and hid the mud in the fields below. He laid a hand on the stone wall of one of the terraces. It was true as a spirit level, cupping the shining mud as it snaked along the valley side.

He climbed again, his path following the course of a dried-up gully, too steep to terrace, whose waters had been taken to irrigate the rice. He passed the last terrace, narrow as a window box but with the same pale mud clasping the rice plants, which were bowed with green droplets of unripe grain.

He was near the top of the Hog, the path so steep that he could lean forward to touch it. The terraces were laid out below him like contour lines on an army map, ducking into the gullies and out like opera boxes onto every promontory. At last he looked at his house.

It nestled so cosily. The houses were ranged in an arc around the village yard, and his was in the perfect place – neither at the ends nor the middle of the arc. He was moved by its patchwork roof. He thought he could see the darker bit of mud where he had mended the front wall.

Behind the houses were private plots where the villagers grew beans, herbs and a few flowers to sell in the town. Fraser squinted at the place where he might have his own plot, though the land at present was used by Wang Dechen.

Beyond the village, acres of rice plants were deep green in the valley bottom but paler on the valley sides. Down the valley, the twenty or thirty roofs of Market Village were dark under the shade trees. Beyond was the road to the Chinese town, then the river, then the almost vertical slopes of the mountains on the far bank.

The villagers were using the rest day to work on their private crops. They were too small to recognize from this height: Fraser only knew them by the houses they entered or the private plots they tended. He thought how they might be glancing across at his house, or walking past it, or just vaguely thinking, 'That belongs to Fraser.'

Perhaps Joy would hear about his house, and come back.

He walked cautiously to the top of slope. He squatted

down for a minute, wondering if he had been seen, then quickly crossed the Hog. He wanted to look at the Chinese town.

At first he saw only a jumble of roofs. The town had grown enormously, dozens of stained concrete houses filling the slope above the river, steep alleys tumbling between them and a haze of coal smoke above.

He sat on the Hog and watched. Five hundred feet below, buffalo grazed in the clinic field. Then came the clinic buildings, then the ground fell steeply away and the town was grey-black roofs tipped at all angles, stepping down towards the river.

He tried to remember his route on that first day when he arrived from Korea, but too much time had passed and too many new buildings had been added as the town expanded from the riverfront.

He listened to the roaring of trucks on the river road, the tinkle of bicycle bells, and the voice of a wonderful young woman from the loudspeakers at every corner. There was nothing to stop him going to the town, and he had the chit to cash at the post office.

He came down the ridge. For a few minutes he stared through the barbed-wire fence around the buffalo field, just as Madame Tao had done the first day he saw her. The clinic seemed busier, and one of the derelict buildings had been repaired, with whitewash over the bullet-holes and glass in the windows.

On the pavement outside the clinic, two old men were bending and stretching in the sun. He remembered how he had come here to beg for his release from the village, but had been forced to build his own life with his own house, and could now be proud. He hurried from that sinister place and into the narrow alleys.

A bustle of people pushed by. Children in uniform marched past with brooms, off somewhere to sweep a yard. Steam billowed from an open door: it was a noodle kitchen, where stout ladies in white toiled their strong arms in the vats.

He ducked down a side alley. At once everything was domestic detail. An old woman on a stool was shelling peas. Cabbage leaves were threaded on strings to dry. Two girls were skipping as they had in his home town. Chickens pecked at the path, and were wafted away by a woman drying melon seeds on a mat. A parrot swung in a straw hoop.

He came to a little square, no more than a patch of broken concrete at the meeting of four alleys. There were pansies in pots on the balconies. On the steepest of these alleys an old woman sold tea from the open door of her house. With shy gestures he bought a cupful and squatted on the kerb. The tea had cost him an hour's pay. There was river sand in the bottom, but no greenish tinge or strands of weed like the water in the village.

Five or six women with shopping baskets stood opposite him on the concrete, watching a man in a scarlet jacket. Fraser squinted to see. The man held a staff topped by a birdcage. Attached to the cage was a small tray with a handful of sticks. It was some kind of fortune-telling, because from time to time he opened the cage and a little bird hopped out to pick up one of the sticks. Its choice was discussed with much laughter.

Fraser walked down towards the river, the concrete

apartment blocks of three and four storeys giving way to older houses of wood. The ground was suddenly sticky. It was blood from a man skinning eels.

The lane opened out into a bustling market, much bigger than the one in Market Village. There were repairers of shoes and umbrellas, wart removers, and a rat killer with a stuffed rat on a pole. Stalls sold chestnuts, roast dog, baked sweet potatoes, steamed rice in banana leaves, and heaps of vegetables specked with toilet paper from the fertilizer. Miao women sat among bales of greenery: he recognized one who had a stall in Market Village.

Shoulder poles tangled, there were shouts and laughter, and Fraser retreated to a corner where dogs, lizards, doves, snakes and kittens crouched in baskets, waiting to be eaten. He stared idly at a stall of mops, made from the relentless blue and green of recycled clothes, noting the rare splashes of colour, perhaps from a child's dress. He loitered by stalls of leaf tobacco, bicycle parts, bits of linoleum, sickles, trowels and odd lengths of rope.

There was a flight of broad stone steps. They seemed to be the backbone of the town, and he followed them downhill from the market square, past the small shops and at last to the river.

A square of stone slabs opened out at the bottom of the steps, and a concrete jetty made a landing place for the river boats. This square was also the end of the river road: half a dozen wagons were unloading, and passengers struggled from a bus with boxes and cages. He could climb aboard, but it would only take him to another part of China. Besides, he needed to fix his roof.

Along the riverfront, wooden houses waded on stilts into the shallows, with little fishing boats drawn up beneath them and fish drying on the balconies, threaded through the gills like washing.

He stared at the familiar grey water. The river was a mile or two upstream of the Miao valley, yet it seemed wider. Submerged rocks raised it in lumps, and larger rocks broke through, even in midstream, cutting a wake like a speedboat.

He was tired now. He turned back uphill and came to a little square, with two trees and a man selling roast chestnuts. The trees were full of birdcages. At first he thought the birds were for sale, but each was attended by a proud old man.

More old men arrived, each with a bird in its cage of split bamboo. They hung the cages on one of the low branches, and then stood smoking and talking, gesturing at the birds with their pipe stems or standing in complacent admiration.

They soon roused themselves because the teacher bird had come. It was placed in the centre of the square, with the other birds ranged around, cloths over their cages except for a little slit so they could see the teacher. It had a specially fine song which its students had come to learn. With much formality, coins were handed to its owner.

This was a beautiful town. He didn't know if the old men came every day with their birds, only that they came every rest day, as he did for years.

After New Year the alleys were littered with spent firecrackers. In summer, the best place was down by the river. In the back yard of a house by the market, generations of pigs grew and then vanished: when they could rest their chin between their forefeet on the top of the wall, gazing wisely at passers-by, he knew they were doomed.

He never learned the language, but managed regular purchases for Wang Dechen: salt, chillies, and a kind of sweet, made from sugar and pig fat, that Wang's sister loved. In exchange she gave him crickets.

He liked the crickets, but liked their cages more. She wove them of rice straw, the size of a fist and neat as a bird's nest, and he put them in a sack in the corner of his room, adding each cage as its insect died after a few days of vigorous song. In winter the crickets lived longer but sang less, only rousing themselves on rest day afternoons, singing faster and faster as his house grew warm.

Perhaps she could hear their song faltering, because Wang Dechen was always ready with a replacement. He liked to work alone on the valley sides, where he had a special skill with the terraces, their tall fragile banks, the grit that washed into them, and the seeping unreliable streams that kept them damp. There were lots of crickets there, though in winter they hid among the stones.

His sister, though, was only a dim figure passing behind Wang as he stood in his doorway, or hurrying to the latrine in the evening with a cloth over her head. In all those years Fraser only saw her once in daylight.

A wagon had arrived in Market Village with bundles of bamboo poles, because all across China it was Bird-killing Day. There was so much excitement that she came to her door, hanging on Wang Dechen's arm, blinking against the light, her pale mad face as round as a pan of fat. But Young Tao and the other children began to shout and hit cooking pots, and she shrank inside, big hands pressed to her cheeks.

The little birds were chased with poles across the valley until they fell exhausted and were beaten to death. Young Tao was surprised: it seemed that flying was hard, like swimming. Next summer there was a plague of insects, so the birds were never attacked again.

The great famine hardly touched them. Starving people wandered up from the town, but they were too weak to cause trouble and staggered away to eat bark in the hills, or fell asleep until they died. Anyway, at harvest-time the police came.

They watched the crop and the villagers. They supervised the harvest, and at night they carried the threshing box from the headman's house and slept around it in the empty storehouse.

The sergeant was the same policeman who had first brought Fraser to the village, and had beaten Old Tao in the station yard. He was still lean, but now had a little hard paunch. His senior officer shook Fraser's hand and said, 'I studied your language, thank you. My name is Zhao. I am healthy. And you?' But Fraser hated to speak English.

As the villagers loaded the bags of rice onto a handcart the policemen boasted about how bad it was in the town. Families were letting their oldest and youngest die, and there was talk of cannibalism in the poorer streets by the river.

But the policemen wouldn't walk in the muddy fields, so Fraser had shown the villagers how they could scrape off the rice grains between finger and thumbnail as they weeded, throwing grain and weeds into the same bag to be sorted later.

With this and their government ration they were hungry but not starving, so the police came back and searched for hidden stores, making them move the midden and prise up the cobbles in the buffalo byre. But their rice was sealed in the clay walls of the houses, or baked in balls of clay and hidden in their roofs, or buried under the bottom of fence posts, a lump of dung on top to confuse the rats, and was never found.

Tao grumbled about the change of mealtimes: they only ate in daylight, watching for police raids.

Fraser had a favourite corner in the town, where the tea was cheap and rows of ragged picture books lay along the pavement. Every rest day afternoon he squatted contented on his heels, sipping tea and thumbing through a story of love and betrayal.

Nearby, the barbers stood by their chairs, their mirrors on nails in the wall. They wouldn't cut Fraser's hair: he was the dirty long-nose who lived with the dirty Miao. Instead Fraser went to the barber in Market Village, afterwards combing his hair with lamp oil to kill any lice eggs. This barber always wanted to crop him to the scalp, but Fraser was proud of his longer hair, which showed he was clean like the Chinese.

One day, the books were scattered and torn. Their owner leaned against the wall, a bloody rag to his face, while the townsfolk veered away, afraid of catching his bad luck.

Fraser persisted for a few more weeks, although the market grew smaller, confined to essentials, and the stallholders were watchful. Only the animal vendors continued to flourish, supported by their trade with the clinic.

As usual Fraser felt he could be invisible. He walked with rounded shoulders so that he could duck under this trouble, even under the new voice through the loud-speakers: instead of the wonderful young woman, it belonged to someone angry and male.

He began to see roving groups of youngsters with red armbands, and at last chose to spend his Sundays in the valley. Occasionally he walked to the top of the Hog and looked down on the town, puzzling over the angry voice. Weeks passed before he discovered that it belonged to a cousin of Madame Fei, the director of the clinic.

7

For a little while Madame Fei's father had been rich. Beijing had decided that China should be self-sufficient in rubber, and sites were chosen downstream from the town, where the river had already fallen hundreds of metres and grown fat and slow among subtropical swamps. Local farmers were not consulted. Saplings, planted too far up the valley sides, starved in the thin soil and were nibbled by deer.

But first the land had to be cleared. Madame Fei had been raised in the south, where her father was a ganger in a building company run by his brother. She used her growing influence and he was put in charge of the eager young volunteers.

He worried about everything, including what should be done with the cleared undergrowth. No one in the Party had considered the matter. They suggested bonfires, or giving it to the locals for firewood. But among the tangle of worthless scrub were hundreds of pine trees. They were inaccessible for the peasants, but the peasants didn't have a Party tractor.

He winched them to the dirt road where a local builder took them away by night. He already considered himself rich when, at the bottom of a dozen fetid ravines, he found teak and tropical oak.

Her parents built a concrete house on the river road, with a television and amazing plastic curtains, embossed with yellow flowers. Such luck couldn't come again to her stupid father. Her mother grew sour with recrimination and consulted a master of feng shui, who found that the front door, although built to a standard size, was a finger's width smaller than the back. Naturally their luck was leaving faster than it arrived.

At once the front door was screened behind a fence of woven reeds, and everyone came and went via a muddy path down the side of the house. It was too late. Her mother grew shrill and thin, ate herself up and died, and Madame Fei came to take care of her father. He briefly embraced her, and was next seen scraping at the useless garden.

She wasn't a natural housekeeper, and remembered her cousin. Like thousands of other Chinese he had been shipped to the town to dilute the local tribes with more tractable citizens. He was sixteen, lived in a worker's hostel and was too surly to argue about anything.

He arrived with his clothes in a shopping bag, stared briefly at the old man, then turned to the flickering television, one of the few hangovers from their days of prosperity. He discovered a rifle in the spare bedroom, a Japanese infantry weapon which Madame Fei had found behind a filing cabinet in the clinic. It amused her to see the boy's casual swagger as he crouched like a sniper at their kitchen window.

There was no ammunition, but he surprised her by finding a source in the town police. These rounds, standard government issue, were a smaller calibre than their Japanese equivalent and tumbled as soon as they left the muzzle. They were impossible to aim but deadly at close range, tearing horrible holes in the fence posts around the kitchen garden.

The boy had picked up a trick from his police friends: as he practised his marksmanship he pushed a live round into his right ear as a muffler. The crack of the rifle echoed around the concrete walls, and during one such session Madame Fei moved back to the clinic.

The boy's name was Huang Hua. Later he became one of the famous cannibals of the Cultural Revolution.

By then Huang was twenty-three and jobless. He was recently back from Kunming, where he drove delivery trucks for the summer. One night, walking home drunk, he had found himself a dozen paces behind a woman. He cleared his throat, thinking how she would hear him.

He began to seek out women, even when they weren't going his way. Bus stations in the outskirts were the best, and he made special journeys in the late evening to follow women into the back streets, coughing to show his presence. Sometimes he ran noisily up behind them and continued on past. Once he jumped in front of a woman, laughing into her shocked face.

One night, watching at his local bus station, he was pushed into an alley and beaten up by three militia men. He came home the next day.

He was quick to understand the new order. On his uncle's television he saw the energy of the Cultural Revolution, the huge crowds, the youngsters hailing the Chairman. He watched the uproar spreading into the countryside as students dispersed to challenge the right-ists. His mouth grew small with satisfaction. Now they would pay.

He hung around the town, watching for change. There was a tea stall where students gathered in the holidays. He talked to them, but found only anxiety. They were not from peasant families. Wouldn't the Guards attack them? Huang returned to the shameful concrete house, but in the morning he had the answer. They must form their own Red Guard unit.

They acquired a uniform, their standard blue suits supplemented by a red armband and – Huang's invention – the tiniest red button on the jacket pocket. Later, in solidarity with the peasants, they changed their cloth caps for straw.

The tea stall gave them tea, cakes and pickled vegetables. Even the police had a gruff tolerance. Huang made a leather sling for his rifle.

Most mornings he arrived with a new slogan, taken from the television news. They daubed it on walls, paraded it through the streets, howled it in the faces of office workers.

They would link arms and corral a crowd of passers-by, lecturing them with the new truth. They occupied the reception room at the Party offices until Huang was permitted to shout it through the loudspeakers that dominated the town. They marched down the hill to the river and let the swift water snatch it away on paper boats.

It was true that the boats would merely spin along the shore while the red paper melted into the water.

Nevertheless, the Guards still sang their defiant chants: somehow, although the message was red pulp among the slabs of the landing stages, it would nevertheless carry through all the river's windings to its destination, capitalist Hong Kong. The Guards returned triumphant to the tea stall.

There were no girls, however. Girls joined the unit, usually two friends together, and enthralled them with their Loyalty Dance at the street-corner shrine to Chairman Mao. But in a few days they left, and the squad became thoughtful.

It was a judgement. It meant that they were wasting their time with slogans when elsewhere the Guards were torturing bourgeois rightists and counter-revolutionaries. But they themselves were the sons of shopholders, teachers, Party bureaucrats. What could they do?

Huang again supplied the answer, having remembered his mad cousin. Madame Fei hated him, as she hated everyone, but had once told him about the slaughter of the clinic buffalo, and who had done it and why.

The villagers stopped work as a score of youngsters strode through the fields. They were waving something red. They were singing or chanting, but as usual the wide fields sucked the sound away.

Huang noticed how their voices were unconvincing under this broad sky. It was even harder in the village. The Miaos were half buffalo, after all, and the Guards were distracted by their tottering houses and the ragged children dirty as beasts. And it was hard to breathe. But they had come to fight the Four Olds, and bravely chanted their new slogan against 'old ideas, old culture, old customs, old habits'.

Only the headman dared to come out. He was disconcerted by these children. He had trouble understanding their standard speech, and his bull neck was useless because they looked at him but didn't see, waving their red books and chanting. And there were girls, so pretty and clean and angry.

Their leader stepped forward. He had a town accent which the headman could understand but hardly believe. He wanted to see where the buffalo was kept.

First the headman licked the clumsy paintings from the wall of the byre, then ate the little clay figurines. He stepped carefully into the midden, like a man entering a cold lake, and slowly sat down. He was draped in the buffalo reins, and the tin tray that Tao had used for a shrine was twisted and hung around his neck.

He weighed more than any two of the Guards, but said nothing as they screamed in his face. Passive as a great beast, he was led from the village, his shrieking family trailing behind.

Here they met the buffalo. It was hauling itself out of the water onto the narrow track while a skinny man, strange-looking even for a Miao, splashed away from them across the field. The Guards were chanting again and the beast grew frightened. It wheeled side-on across the track, stretching its long head and braying, its tail stuck straight out.

Only one of the villagers had used a rifle. In its ineffectual crack he heard Korea. He turned round and saw the dying buffalo wallowing back into the water, its front legs buckling. He cradled the great head until its eyes were dusty.

Tao was impressed. He wanted to see the man who had taken their useless headman.

Great things had happened to Huang Hua. Soon after the raid on the village, a squad of Red Guards at last arrived from the city. Its leader shaved his head like a poor peasant and never smiled. Nevertheless, he at once merged his team with the others and looked to Huang for instructions.

The new group brought new rigour. First the Guards cornered anyone in glasses, then anyone with a briefcase. Protests were answered with a blow. People would be searched for books, and their choices were always wrong: any non-fiction was counter-revolutionary, any fiction was bourgeois.

A young man had a yellow novel, printed in Beijing. Huang vaguely knew his father, yet he was stripped, beaten and driven into the river with fists and stones. Perhaps he drowned.

Huang and his friends learned city tricks. If a victim shielded himself from a beating, you simply asked him to stop. You could demand that shoes were removed.

On television, Huang had seen the torture called the aeroplane – a man's wrists pulled back and up until he bowed to his knees. But the city Guards had a new style: the wrists were tied behind the back with electrical wire, then levered up with a stick between the shoulder blades.

Their first execution was overdue. Huang told his family to stay away.

8

The Party had agreed to replace the dead buffalo, and Tao knew of an animal in Market Village. It was young, but by next spring would be strong enough to plough.

It belonged to an old man who might be his uncle. They would exaggerate its age and therefore its value, just as Tao had minimized the age of the feeble old buffalo that the Guards had shot. Fraser was still boring in his grief, so Tao went alone, despite the sack of garlic he was carrying to sell in the town.

'You woman,' said his uncle. He never forgot that Tao had moved to his wife's village, against the custom, instead of bringing her here. 'You woman, who can't protect your buffalo.'

'Not from the Guards, uncle,' said Tao, looking around for informers. 'Anyway, because of that day we both get fat.'

Tao's uncle was the richest man in the valley, the only one with two wives, the eldest tottering on bound feet the size of fists. He had been greatly helped by the Revolution.

The Reds had insisted that all cultivable land must be used for agriculture, so even the Miao burial mounds were levelled. One man killed himself for grief, another dug up his family, recently dead of a fever, and doused them with lamp oil, throwing handfuls of soya beans on the burning bodies so that even the bones were consumed.

A few families started new mounds, small and secret, on the valley sides. But most wanted their graves in plain view, and used odd corners of the village, or their house yards, or even their own floors. Ideologically correct Miao, such as the headman of Market Village, had no such problems, taking their dead to the Chinese graveyard between the town and the dump, where the ceremonies involved no animal sacrifice or references to the old gods.

But the headman also allowed food grown on the old mound sites to be mixed with the rest: the ancestors, still indignant, sent maladies that only Old Tao's uncle could address. He even dispensed native medicine to one or two Chinese women in the town, although they insisted that he come to them. The headman tried to intercept any payments, but couldn't prevent villagers donating food or helping the old man with his ceaseless building projects.

He had the biggest house in the valley, extra rooms proliferating from the sides and back of his original home, which was his consulting room and must preserve its view down the valley. From their chair, the old man's clients could see straight down the track of light which lay on the stream as it emerged from their fields and ran towards the river. It was such a perfect view that Tao gave his sarcastic smile.

Market Village consisted of three semicircles of houses, corresponding to the three slave-owning families who had built it. Each enclosed an area of packed earth. The largest held the weekly market from which the settlement took its name, but Tao's uncle lived in the smallest and most elegant of these arcs.

The old man liked to muse with his patients about whether these arcs mimicked the new moon or a buffalo's horns. He would never indulge such habits under Tao's ironic eye, but there was anyway no disagreement about the purpose of the arc, which was duplicated in the little village further up the valley, on which the three arcs of Market Village so decisively turned their backs: each house must face down a valley, preferably over water, to allow good energy its clearest entrance and exit.

The old man's house stood at the apex of the arc, and therefore enjoyed the most propitious aspect. A beautiful shade tree bent over his roof, and he put rice in its lower forks to please its lazy, kindly female spirit, who lived there as a coven of sparrows. But he had recently turned eighty, and grown afraid of death.

When Tao was a boy in Market Village, his uncle taught him the rituals of the buffalo cult. But this was before the Revolution. With freedom came the freedom to disagree. The older man inclined towards fasts and all-night meditation, whereas Tao favoured ribbons and raids. Instead of honouring the buffalo like his uncle, Tao saw it as a fat lowland creature, slow as the Chinese and as ripe for mockery.

They split definitively over a guru called the Teacher, a devotee of the gods of potholes and sharp bends. Soon after his marriage, and against his uncle's demands, Tao had walked to a Yi village in the next province where the Teacher had ended his brief career by wallowing in the latrine for a week, laughing at the villagers who laughed at him, until he was hauled out by a delegation of the outraged women.

Tao found the village abandoned, destroyed by its own infection of black pranks – roofs burned, women molested, and at last a buffalo slaughtered and its entrails thrown to rot in the well. The fields and people had been absorbed by surrounding hamlets, and the Teacher's hut flattened. But there was a pile of painted rocks where he had been driven from the village with sticks and laughter, to die laughing in the hills.

Tao took a ragged banner from one of the houses. It showed concentric circles like a target. Inside each ring was a crowd of drawings and ideographs, which he studied all his life. The outermost ring was shit, which even animals avoid. Inside that was the ring of beasts, then of men, then of gurus, including the Teacher, then of earthly spirits, then spirits of the air. At the centre was an eye, which sees the whole universe and (some say) thereby creates it.

Now his old uncle led him to the buffalo. It was clumsy and strong, testing its new muscles against the tethering post. The old man feared that the animal would be mocked with paint and girlish ribbons if it moved to the village, but he could do nothing. Most of his wealth came from trading the buffaloes he worshipped, and he wanted the Party's money.

Tao said, 'It's skinny, uncle.'

'Because its bones are big.'

There was no need to haggle. They need only decide by how much they could cheat the Party. Nevertheless, Tao smelled the creature's coat, lifted each hoof, stroked the small buds of its horns, and at last put his hand inside the old man's coat, where they counted fingers until a price was fixed. Even then he couldn't keep quiet: 'It has an angry look, uncle. Very angry. It will kill the village children.'

'Not yours, anyway,' said the old man, too unhappy to watch his words.

Tao walked on into town, going first to the Party offices to see if his chit had arrived. He was leaving empty-handed when a man burst past him, followed by a gang of Red Guards.

Huang himself had stopped the man outside the Party offices. He was carrying foreign books and a pipe stamped Made In Hong Kong, yet dared to smile as he fled inside. The Guards didn't hesitate. He was dragged into the street, where Huang hit him with his rifle butt.

Placards saying 'Ox Demon' and 'Capitalist Roader' appeared round his neck. New ones, appropriate to his crimes, were at once composed under Huang's supervision. They read 'Lackey of Capitalism' and 'Imperialist Running Dog'. For the first time a police patrol arrived to protect the Guards.

And the run down to the river was perfect. He was hauled first to the market square and bowed down among the cabbage leaves, the wire on his wrists allowing even the frailest girls to lever him over until his blood dripped onto the cobbles.

His confession done, he was harried down the hill, past the small shops and tea stalls, wanting to fall on the stone steps but held up by the aeroplane, then halted halfway down to repeat his admission. Then it was on to the landing stages.

There were great metal hoops for tying up boats, and stone slabs for unloading. Huang swung his rifle like someone chopping wood. The man lay across a fat chain that coiled into the water. At last he stretched luxuriously and wet himself.

Huang didn't want to leave the body. It was a great prize, heavy as treasure. He took a handsome ballpoint pen but left unsatisfied.

The townsfolk, though, were less confused. Executions had always brought the superstitious with their bread, and the more terrible the criminal the more potent his blood. Police manuals warned against greater indignities, reminding officers of the old adage: '*Yi nao bu nao, yi xin bu xin*' – 'Feed brain with brain, feed heart with heart'. A constant guard was recommended.

But the victims of the Cultural Revolution lay unprotected. As the fighting spread, rumours began about the landing stages, and what the dead endured before the river carried them away.

9

It was late summer when the next batch of Guards arrived, and the villagers had opened their doors to the evening cool. There was a thickening of the darkness, a murmuring, and then figures in their doorways.

Fraser followed Wang Dechen into the yard, covering his eyes, looking away, pretending to squint at the flashlights. The Guards smashed crockery and chairs, but since the last raid the shrines had vanished, and there were no more paintings of buffaloes on their hind legs, no whips or bones or embroidered tassels. The important bits of their old murdered animal were eaten or hidden, and the meat had been sold in the town, where the Chinese would eat anything, even the grey muscle of a working buffalo.

The Guards checked for tattoos. The women were sent indoors and the men had to strip. Even Tao could smile: they were searching for a Miao tradition that didn't exist. But as Fraser was dragged forward he knew he was finished. Even the villagers were shocked at his hairy flesh. A moment of silence was followed by incredulous shrieks from the Guards.

He glimpsed a blurred movement and fell to his knees. A warm pulse spread from the side of his head, flowing out of his ankles and leaving him sick. His arms were pulled back and upwards so that he was first lifted to his feet and then bowed forward. Questions were screamed at him, but he struggled to understand their standard speech and wondered if he would die.

He heard a woman's voice. Much later he realized it was Wang Dechen's sister. She said that Fraser was a peasant, come to China to learn Mao Tse-tung thought: he wanted to work among the poor peasants and then take Mao Tse-tung thought to the round-eyes. Everyone in the village, she said, had agreed to this.

She was silenced with a punch, but the Guards were arguing among themselves.

For six months Fraser travelled with the Guards among the hill tribes, carrying dried pork to stuff down the throats of the Hiu people, who were Muslim.

Part prisoner, he was also part mascot. He frightened the tribals with his hairy arms, and was in turn disgusted by their superstitions. There were too many. Their numbers made them stupid. He learned the chant against the Four Olds and grew sick with the dust of fetishes kicked along village streets past shrieking women and men silent with anger or grief.

Amongst the Yi he gave the aeroplane to anyone identified as upper caste, bending them down until they swept the animal pens with their faces. He took the tablets of their dead from behind the kitchen stoves and made their own priests smash them. These priests were whipped on the soles of their feet until they directed the Guards to the cave in the mountains where the village ancestors held their conclave, and from where the musty paraphernalia was rolled down the slopes.

The Zhuang live in raised houses and use human

figurines in their worship. Their sorcerers had to destroy their own shrines, as did the shamans of the Yao, who worship animals.

Once, standing in a village square, he saw two men across the fields. They were carrying a box as tall as themselves. He hesitated but then called out, and the Guards raced after them.

The box was like an open coffin. Inside was a bundle of old straw threaded with bones and beads, which the two men died to protect. Soon it burned among the maize, its smoke drifting back over the village and the wailing women.

Occasionally he was questioned. The Guards had a little English, he had a little standard speech, and in time he learned that his village, and the town, and all the surrounding county had been closed to foreigners since the war against the Japanese. He couldn't explain his presence there and was beaten.

He didn't resent this treatment, which the Guards administered to almost everyone they met, only caring about his army boots, treasured and mended for years in the Miao valley, which the Guards threw away in their rage.

They came to a Buddhist monastery. While they smashed its wooden screens a monk was held by four of the Guards. At last Fraser recognized Young Tao.

He had left the village a year before. Tao had tried to raise him in the buffalo cult, and took him on half-hearted searches for medicinal plants. Young Tao learned a little about encouraging the animal's strength and protecting it from spells, but saw Tao's uncertainty and his preference for sitting in the buffalo byre expounding on the grand themes of man and animal.

Even here the youngster was unconvinced. While Tao declaimed or painted its horns, the buffalo was stupid as a wall, its excrement untimely.

One stifling afternoon, working alone, Young Tao noticed the ripples widening away from him across the flooded field. Two weeks later he cooked a little rice and walked far upriver to the monastery in a side valley in the mountains. He kept stopping on the path, filled with an unexpelled sigh. Once he sank to his hands and knees under the weight of revelation, a guest of the small stones.

At the monastery he didn't speak for a week, until a master hit him across the shoulders during meditation. Young Tao picked the man up, put him down, and then tore a window from its hinges. This anger was also new. It filled him like his glimpses of the Way, and the masters understood and called him Brother Buffalo.

He worked the monastery farm and saw Old Tao's animal cult from the other side. Instead of spells and busyness, he noted the silence of animals and their complete passions.

But his element was air, and to an extent stones. They drew him into journeys through the hills. Here he had a toiling walk, because he was wading through air. When he stood still the sky again laid its foot on him, pressing him to the ground where the air puts its mouth around every pebble. His dreams were of flying, falling, and treading water high above the village.

When the monastery burned it was a liberation. He watched cross-legged, blood running into his eyes, and thought, 'After all, it's turning into air.'

He returned to the village, the smell of burning still in his clothes, and Tao took him at once to the young buffalo. It had grown enough to need a thicker nose-rope, and Tao had plaited the end of its old rope to the end of the new. In the evenings he tied the old rope to the wall. Night by night, if the animal wanted to lie down, it must pull the new rope a little further through its nostrils.

Tao had never managed a young buffalo before, and owed this and other tricks to his uncle, who still worried about the dignity of the beast he had sold, and found many excuses to walk up from Market Village.

His uncle hoped for an ally in Young Tao. A sometime Buddhist must agree that the One is superior to the Many: he need only be persuaded that the buffalo was its emblem. The old man would therefore pat the buffalo's head and nod significantly. A buffalo's armoured forehead represents the concentrated will, he believed, the superior man focused on a single purpose.

Young Tao said nothing, but Tao laughed. A buffalo's forehead is split, after all, sweeping out into two horns. Clearly it signifies the double mind, which enjoys contradiction, irony, new things.

His uncle said that celebrating the buffalo for its mind is like celebrating the rat for its strength.

Tao asked why his uncle worshipped an animal that

he disrespected. Clearly a buffalo represents the highest awareness, which is awareness of self.

His uncle said that a buffalo thinks that the butcher is bringing his dinner.

Tao said that the tips of a buffalo's horns point back at each other, showing how a man must critically judge his own thoughts, not be swept up by them.

His uncle said that a buffalo has no thoughts.

Tao couldn't explain what his uncle anyway knew, that Tao saw no contradiction between mocking the buffalo and honouring it. So he said that wit is more important than strength, as anyone knew who didn't live too far down the valley. The Miao are mountain people, or should be, kept alert on the keen air, not stupefied like the Chinese.

The old man said that Tao had been born and raised in Market Village, and that a buffalo thinks that by dragging the cart he'll escape the driver's whip.

Tao stammered slightly and agreed that the buffalo is stupid. In fact, its horns only confuse it, in the same way that most men have heads that are only big enough for one idea. But a clever man can turn around inside his head and watch himself. Irony, shading into farce, is his sign. His icons are a buffalo on its hind legs and a man walking on his hands, head in his trousers, genitals flapping. This was the message of the Teacher.

The old man controlled his anger and glanced at Young Tao. He said that the Lord Buddha showed that a man chooses the single mind at all the important moments of his life: in the making of babies, when the mind shrinks to fit through the eye of the penis, and in the killing of our enemy, when we are wise as our weapons.

Tao said that the Lord Buddha had taught peace, and was too fat to make babies. Yes, we share functions with the beasts, such as anger or lust, but nobody wants to be stupid for ever – except perhaps their old headman with his Shanghai whisky.

His uncle said that a buffalo's two horns come together at the forehead, signifying how the wise man creates unity out of the world's diversity.

Tao, laughing openly, said that the unity of the forehead deludes certain people into ignoring the multiplicity of the horns, just as they think there is a single explanation for the whole world – usually some religion or philosophy. In fact no man can grasp the world, nor even China, nor even the stone in his shoe.

Tao's uncle grew tired, and couldn't walk to the village. Young Tao had been no help. He was only interested when the old man talked about the Miao wars of fifty years before, when heads were lopped off and hearts eaten, and a man must feel the One flowing down his arm or be butchered like a beast.

Or else when he recalled the Christian missionaries, who showed that everyone was wrong to think that white people slept standing up like horses: it took Fraser's arrival, however, and Old Tao's sharp eyes, to reveal that whites didn't also have four testicles.

Most of all, Young Tao liked to hear about the years just before he was born, when the Japanese had occupied the town and took pot shots at the Miao villages from their machine-gun nest on top of the Hog, and how the Miao had their turn on the Hog, watching as the Chinese army returned.

The Japanese had retreated to the clinic, which they had built and where they brought prisoners from across south China. Near the end of the battle a Japanese soldier escaped up the Hog, and the Miao harried him into the valley and did a number of things before and after his death, even though he was a coward and therefore bad medicine.

Young Tao acknowledged the One, as we all must. But instead of finding it down a gunsight, he looked for the One which is everything – not a narrowing of the mind but its greatest widening, where we leave the treadmill of desire and disappointment, which are halves of a greater whole. Anyway he would never oppose Tao, who always won because he found these arguments funny.

The old man died during the winter and was angry to the end. He should have been more forthright over the getting of babies, he decided. Tao's smirking had robbed the family of sons.

He, on the other hand, had many children. As he lay dying, the household filled with squabbling relatives. He roused himself and told them to melt down the ceremonial brass tips used on the horns of his oldest bull: they must be made into a single plate for its forehead. His family preferred not to understand, and did nothing.

10

Next spring the villagers were greatly excited by a little blue aeroplane. It flew regularly along the Miao valley, and feathers or scraps of paper fluttered down behind it.

One afternoon it left thousands of grey beetles struggling in the flooded fields. Tao declared they had been generated by its propeller cutting through the smoke from his fire, because that morning he had burned some old clothes, which naturally contained sweat and oil from his skin.

Next day they heard that a truck from the clinic had appeared at Market Village an hour before the flight. Men in white coats had fanned out across the valley to wait for the insects.

Fired by this humiliation he took Young Tao to the tiny airstrip, recently cleared from a cattle meadow downriver. A new tent, still with its creases from storage, flapped in the dusty wind. Inside, a mechanic leaned from his chair and watched them approach the plane.

Young Tao's breath was stopped. At the monastery they had pointed out the spirits of the air, which are often visible at sunset, and his first interest was to search the wings for traces, which he supposed might be filmy like shed skin. Instead he saw the scratched perspex windows and an oil smear by the exhaust like the smear under a puppy's tail.

The wings shaped the air like a tongue. Or perhaps it

was like one of Old Tao's spells. Or they rushed along the airstrip until they had gathered enough air, like a man herding geese. He circled the plane until the mechanic came and showed him the engine.

Tao left them talking and walked to the town, where he went most days, ever since he had crept to that first body left by Huang and his squad.

Beijing had demanded an end to such killings. The town police, unsure of their strength, merely asked that the Red Guards attack only each other.

But this meant taking sides, and the police chose badly. At that time, the moderate Guards held the town and the radicals seemed mere terrors of the countryside, only strong enough to persecute the tribes. When radicals were captured and dragged to the landing stages to die, it seemed a useful first step towards order.

But the moderates were now outflanked. From their colleagues in neighbouring towns the police learned of a gathering army of radicals. They prepared to change sides.

Fraser, camped with the radicals, was pestered by language students. His English-speaking voice hadn't aged: it was still gruff and shy, cramped by accent, so he escaped among the dozens of tents and tried to understand the speeches against the rightists of the Red Guard moderates.

On the sixth day they broke camp and marched away singing. Fraser was carrying the big tent for his squad and lagged behind as they crested a slope. When he saw the familiar river, with the town in the crook of its elbow, radical Guards already streamed through the outskirts.

An army platoon defended the clinic bravely, but wouldn't use their firearms. Windows were smashed, the buffaloes were panicked through the streets, and Professor Fei, husband of the clinic director, was left bleeding in an alley. Then the Guards turned to their real target.

By the time Fraser arrived most of the moderates were dead. He advanced with his squad in a flanking movement along the river frontage. They filtered through stinking alleys, past slum houses, naked children and the backs of boat sheds, and suddenly emerged into the open space of the landing stages.

The moderate Guards had relived the last moments of their victims. Driven from their stronghold in the market square, they were harried down the stone steps, past the small shops where so many others had made their confessions, and on to the riverfront. Now a dozen survivors crowded onto the concrete jetty.

They bared their teeth as they looked at the river. It was always cold and fast: now it was fat with snowmelt from the mountains, its muscles bunching against pillars of the jetty, and offered no escape.

Fraser was suddenly buffeted. The Guards were pulling someone from a side alley. He had been hiding among the rats and rubbish, but couldn't disguise the shaved head of a moderate. Fraser twisted the rifle from his hands. It was Huang, the Guard who had shot his buffalo.

They applied the aeroplane, using the honest radical style. There were no elaborate wires and levers, just a sturdy Guard on each arm to steer him out onto the landing stages. A great howl rose from their comrades. Huang was a famous killer, and his death big medicine.

But here the radicals paused. They had usually been victims of the ritual killings, not instigators, and were now uncertain.

A slim figure emerged from the crowd. It was Old Tao, confident and quick. With a nod to Fraser, he led them to a particular confluence of chains. Once shackles for boats, they now restrained the dying.

As always Old Tao was deft. Fraser had never seen the cutting of live muscle, which opens like jelly.

Huang only frowned, staring at his tormentors, although his hands shook. He was sick with killing, having recently returned from Wuxuan, centre of the cannibal madness, where he had learned to apply the following tortures: hanging up the pigs, flying hammer with oil, bats climbing on the wall, and rolling dragon holding a post. A little girl had said, 'No, seventh uncle, do not hurt me,' but that evening, like most evenings, a trembling stallholder had given him new canvas shoes, because the old ones were sodden with blood.

Fraser put the rifle to Huang's head, then changed his mind. He walked back into the alleys, the way they had come. He threw the rifle into a sewer and unpinned his Mao Tse-tung badge which, in accordance with radical Guard fashion, was stuck through the flesh over his heart. He put the badge in his pocket for safety's sake. He would sell the big tent but keep the beautiful rucksack with its leather straps and steel buckles. In an hour he was back in his house among the flooded fields.

That night he was disturbed by Tao, who wanted him to share a great prize. The old man ate with glee, his wife with amusement, Young Tao because it saved an argument, and Fraser because it was a kind of belonging. There was nothing left for the rest of the village.

11

Fraser was working on his roof when he saw the last act of the Cultural Revolution in the valley, and afterwards learned the details.

Red Guards appeared at the top of the Hog, and Fraser thought they were coming to revenge his desertion. Instead they marched chanting into Market Village, where they wrecked the house where Old Tao's uncle had recently died, which they rightly suspected of use in the buffalo cult.

. A squad of more thoughtful Guards was visible in the fields. Held by the ears, men and women were led out of Market Village and told to shovel the paths back into the water. All peasants were lazy: the paths were an excuse to cultivate less land.

At once water rushed through the broken paths into the lower fields, and soon much of the upstream land was drained. Fraser knew that the water would be flooding over the downstream paths, washing mud and seedlings into the river.

But the matter wasn't over. It emerged that the teacher at the one-room school in Market Village had cycled into town to talk to the education officer. Next day a police sergeant arrived to inspect the fields, patting his hard football of a paunch. He had a confidential talk with the senior men, and within a day or two the paths were mended.

This meant the Red Guards were finished, and it also settled something in Fraser. The Guards had told him that the river went to Hong Kong, yet he sat on his roof and looked at the hills around the valley, choosing to stay. He had seen the world a little, had watched men die, and in his absence no one had taken his house.

He spent hours on the roof. The rest of the house was no trouble. It was half-timbered like the Taos', a cage of wooden beams resting on a foot-high wall of rough stones. The gaps between the beams were closed by little walls of clay: lumps of clay regularly fell off, but Fraser could quickly pound them with straw and water and push them back onto their wicker underlay.

The roof, though, was a perpetual task. Even pottering around indoors, he constantly reached up to shut out glints of daylight. The roof tiles were made of clay, long and curved like pipes cut in half lengthways. They lay on wooden battens which ran from a beam at the roof ridge to a beam at each eave. The battens were just far enough apart for tiles to be wedged between them, making dozens of gutters. Other runs of tiles, this time cupped downwards, arced over the battens. At night he grew dizzy as he thought about the tiles stretching over the house, gripped together like hooked hands.

He could reach most of the tiles from indoors, but major repairs took him up on the roof. It was like quicksand or thin ice, and he built a raft of fence posts to spread his weight, padding it with the sacks he still used for a bed. He lifted the scraps of thatch and examined the broken tiles.

Wang Dechen frowned thoughtfully from his doorway, then took him to the stream below Market Village where the Miao dug clay to line their fire pits. Fraser dried the clay into makeshift tiles in the village yard, while Wang frowned and was silent. The tiles dissolved in the first rain.

Now Fraser sat on the sweltering roof and examined his little finger. The Guards had broken it in one of their beatings, and it was set crooked. Despite everything, they were right to ask why he had been brought to the village, and why he was allowed to stay. He had never seen another foreigner in all his years in the valley.

He could dig an oven. It would be a little cave in the bank at the edge of the village. About the size of a bucket would do. It should face down the valley, where the wind usually came from. The wind would blow in through an opening in the bank, up through the oven, and out of a chimney at the top. On a dry, windy day it might be hot enough to bake the tiles.

Fraser preferred to steer clear of the great questions of his life, and continued to feel that way for the next eighteen years.

That autumn the men were resting in the fields when Tao became talkative. He was concerned about women. Communism was good, certainly, and still made great men. He personally had met Commander Ou, who had ended the killings with a single slap, landing in the town with thirty soldiers and hitting the police chief across the face in the market square in front of everybody.

But the Communists who came to the village were poor things. Communism, after all, had nothing to do with Miao customs, which they didn't understand.

What was this, for instance, about equality of the sexes? When had the Miao denied it? Yet the Communists came, they gave their lectures when everyone was tired from working in the fields all day, and for a few days Fraser was sent to plant rice with the women, while Madame Tao, carefully supervised, was allowed to feed the buffalo.

A waste of time. Nobody said that women were bad. It was only that they would never, never say if their blood was flowing. If they admitted it there would be no difficulty. But since it was such a precious secret, what could be done? It was easier just to tell them not to step over the tools, or touch lottery tickets or the buffalo.

Tao fell silent. He said nothing more until he and Fraser were struggling to fix a hopeless, rotted old plough. Suddenly he explained how the male seed curdles the menstrual blood into a foetus, which feeds on the monthly flow until the birth. After that the blood is diverted into milk until the mother is ready to breed again.

Still Fraser didn't understand. A week later, long after everyone else, he realized that Madame Tao was pregnant.

She was a slave from generations of slaves. At night her mother had been locked in great wooden boots and slept in the ashes behind the master's stove. She died when Madame Tao was born.

Paternity was never sure amongst the slave caste of the Miao, but she was called daughter by a tall man who died threshing the rice. He had been tending the blinded buffalo: tethered to a stake, with a canvas hammock to catch its droppings, it dragged a log round and round over the grain, and continued unperturbed after he fainted. In death as in life, his body belonged to the master and wasn't seen again.

In those days the village wasn't really a village. The master, a Yi, occupied the big house where the headman now lived, and an overseer slept with his party of shackled slaves in each of the other houses. One of the overseers fell in love with her, but some infection made her bleed for weeks and she couldn't forgive him.

Communism came early to the county, but changed nothing. Just like the war against Japan, the Revolution seemed an affair of the Chinese. Across China the Reds were conquering town after town, and amongst their own kind they were bold and swift. But the tribes had been persecuted and must therefore be virtuous. When soldiers visited the slave villages it was only to say that, from a Marxist perspective, the system was unsustainable.

From this, though, the slaves learned disobedience. One visited from Market Village, an unheard of dereliction. He had an overseer's whip and chased her around the village. His name was Tao. Next morning their overseers had fled and the master's house was barricaded.

For a week the slaves did no work, while the master and his wife peered from their windows, pale as their own ghosts. One day Tao didn't come to visit her and smoke rose from Market Village. They saw the master and his wife hurrying towards the hills.

Madame Tao followed. She strolled after the old couple as they sweated up the valleys. She sat and smoked above the trail while they groaned under their loaded packs. They called out, but received no answer. During the second night she slid down to their camp and hooked away their shoes with a long stick.

They began to leave their heavier treasures on the path – a bolt of silk or a lacquered box – but she wasn't distracted. In the evenings, when the smell of their food filled the valley, she chewed twigs and thought of her nameless ancestors.

She had forgotten the Reds. They followed the trail of riches and easily overtook the old couple. But, returning through the village with their two prisoners, the soldiers were themselves surrounded.

The slaves had been fighting. All the non-Miao had been driven off, along with some of the Miao from too far away. Wang Dechen's accent was strange but his sister's turban was the right colour: they beat their foreheads on the ground and were allowed to claim a house.

Now the villagers crowded around the landlord and his wife. The soldiers didn't protect their prisoners. There was no point saving people who would anyway be shot.

Killing the old couple took most of the day. They sat on the floor in the storehouse while the villagers rampaged through their house, drinking foreign whisky and smashing the window glass. From time to time the master and his wife had visitors, who entered with mocking humility but soon turned to tears, recrimination and blows.

The bodies were left in the pigpen for a week and the bones and rags then thrown in a ditch. As the slaves marked their freedom, most of these pigs were roasted on bonfires made from the shade tree: Tao had cut it down without asking the other villagers, for which they never forgave him. He saved the last bonfire and the last pig for his wedding.

Before Communism the Miao slaves had bred like beasts, without ratification, and already the Taos had been slipping away into the tall maize, a square of green like a room. With no known ceremony they had to improvise.

She stood on his feet and was walked three times through the house they had commandeered. She rode backwards on the blinded buffalo, which must also be free, at least for today, and worked her cruel heels while Tao held its tail and couldn't run for laughing.

They licked each other's eyeballs and spat in one another's mouth. She covered her eyes and screamed while he pissed from their new windows and doors. They rolled in the dust, biting one another's toes, working from the largest to the smallest, biting so hard that the other must stop to squeal. Hand in hand, leading half the village, they splashed through every flooded field, and thereby made the master's land their own.

In the end, though, Huang's heart wasn't quite enough. Madame Tao only produced a girl.

12

Her name was Mee Yang, but Fraser didn't ask. She slept all day on her mother's back, her face like a dumpling in the embroidered baby-frame that Madame Tao had sewn in her maidenhood. She had beaten the cloth with pig's blood, and it was still stiff and shiny when Tao hooked it down from the roof space at the end of her pregnancy, when it seemed that after all the child might live.

Madame Tao's pink cheeks belied her first grey hairs. She fell asleep in the middle of conversations, the infant blinking over her shoulder.

Then Mee Yang emerged, and Fraser was dazzled. While Madame Tao nodded by the fire he cradled the infant or guided her first steps across the house. He came constantly to the Tao household. For the first time, the villagers had to nag him to go to the fields.

'If he wasn't so ugly I might think he was the father,' said Old Tao.

Young Tao was twenty-three and found it all unmanly. When Mee Yang explored further the round-eye gave her tiny felt shoes, even though children are too light to need footwear. Instead of letting her run naked, Fraser bought her the bottomless trousers, like a cowboy's leggings, that Chinese toddlers wear. Her sex was concentric circles like a raindrop in a pool.

Mee was the only child in the village, and pampered

everywhere. From the time she could clamber over the Taos' threshold she seemed never to rest. Except during the spring hunger, when everyone is sleepy, she was a terror to the chickens and a visitor to every house. Tao watched with patrician pride, hands in his pockets, delighted at the world's latest folly.

Fraser never forgot her first visit. By now he had the best house in the village. There was new paper in the windows, and the metal hinges on his stout front door were slick with grease he had taken from an army truck, ducking between its wheels as it parked for a moment outside the police station and carrying the warm grease all the way home on the end of his cupped fingers.

Even the roof was more or less waterproof: he had spent most of one summer drilling holes in the tiles and binding them to the battens with little hoops made from fencing wire stolen from the buffalo field behind the clinic. He had lain in bed amazed at how the village was so poor: generations of toil on the slates had been ended by a shilling's worth of wire.

Behind the house was his private field, also the best in the village. It had once comprised half of Wang Dechen's plot: Fraser had suggested they work it jointly, and thereafter Wang had come to him every day so that they could stand contemplating the plot as Wang sighed and thought. Some days he had brought a stool.

In the end Fraser had simply taken the land. It was the size of a room and as neat as a button box, with a patch of chrysanthemums, its own compost pit, and compartments for vegetables and herbs, celery and carrot. In late summer he slept among the rows to keep away thieves. He grew suspicious of water from the stream, which was clear as gin and could wash away goodness: it was allowed into his land, but must not run through it.

He had always thought he was stupid, and therefore seemed so, but now his field was famous as his house. Once or twice men walked up from Market Village to stare. They stood smoking in silence, then asked gruff questions – but Fraser told them nothing.

Their common problem was the valley soil, a pan of gritty earth between the gravel of the springs and the pebbles of the river valley. The soul of farming was to turn this earth from pale to dark, and Fraser's secrets all involved scavenging for his compost pit: newspapers from the dump kept it warm in winter and rotted down in summer; in the small hours he rose to steal a handful of droppings from the midden; tea leaves, lifted from rubbish bins behind the tea shops in the town, were brewed a second time then composted; and above all he walked miles through the hills, collecting earth.

He had started close to home. High on the valley sides, above the highest rice terraces, were pads of tough grass, small as pincushions or big as pillows, half-hidden under the larger boulders. Generations of Miao women had left them clipped as carpets, so Fraser secretly lifted them complete. He piled them in a corner of his house but was soon spotted and imitated. He was glad he had acted first, because now the high valley sides were bare.

He ranged further. The county was all limestone, full of caves and screes and disappearing streams. Solitary bushes crouched on the hills, which otherwise wore a pelt of wiry grass with scars of grey rock showing through. A few Miao villages lay in scattered valleys, but only goatherds traversed the uplands.

He could still see landscape like a soldier – range, access, field of fire – but there was no cover here: a squad might filter along the bottom of gullies, following the damp earth where a stream should be, but would at last be exposed on a bald meadow. Sure enough the goatherds saw him.

They were languorous men, leaning on a staff or curled with a pipe in a cup of rocks, watching the round-eye hurry across the countryside, his handsome rucksack weighted with earth. The older men grew indignant at this theft, but the young bachelors – who worked separately – laughed at his furious haste, his burning thief's eyes, and once persuaded him to share their tea.

Fraser sat twitching and impatient while the blackened kettle boiled, and didn't come again: he hated the goats because their sharp teeth and hooves cut the turf until it died and broke away, dusty as a rug, sliding on the grey rock like a rug on a concrete floor.

Fraser lifted the thicker turfs, took dark earth from the bottom of gullies, smelled out leaf mould from pockets in the rocks at the feet of thorn bushes, collected droppings from stone enclosures where the goats were held at night, and stole freshly manured soil from fields around the Miao villages. He kept an oiled-paper bag in his pocket, in case he had to shit away from home.

Years before, Fraser had been the first to stop using the village latrine. There were months of argument, but no headman to enforce the common good: now village land had to survive on dung from the animals, and everyone kept their shit for their private fields. They bought more in the town, where every large building had a public toilet and sold its product. Fraser always went to the Party offices, where the shit was expensive but impressively smelly.

Once he paused by the mirror in the Party's beautiful tiled toilet. He was ageing like a Westerner, his face melting downwards from the eyes: in China, faces shrank back around their cheekbones, so that old people seemed to smile into the sun. He was getting bald.

He hurried back outside and picked up the ladle by the brick-lined tank: it took all day to carry the loaded shoulder pole along the river road, past the graveyard and the town dump, then up through Market Village where the children danced and held their noses.

The night before Mee Yang's visit he had stolen a sack of yellow gravel from the roadworks by the river. He was pouring it into the groove cut in the earth by the rainwater running off his roof. There were similar grooves around every house in the village, and eventually they undermined the walls. Not at his house, though.

He heard a grunt and looked round. Mee-Mee was crouched beside him, prodding the yellow stones. Crouching reminded her of something: urine splashed from her split trousers and ran into the groove.

'Ah, you've christened it,' said Fraser, so surprised that he spoke in English. He reminded her often of this incident, though she was soon old enough to resent it.

By this time Young Tao had begun his great adventures.
First he worked on a river boat, but hated the middle-

aged deckhands in the sweltering corridors who complained about everything, including his inconvenient bulk. He acquired a horror of drowning, and lay awake listening to the water rushing outside the steel plates, thinking how it might burst in, fingers aimed at his throat.

He jumped ship near a Miao village in the lowlands, helping with the rice and maize among leeches and mosquitoes, and wondering where the women went all day. After some weeks they took him to the opium fields.

This was the first time his knees hurt. The poppies grew on a steep hillside in the jungle, and the climb left an ache which lasted the rest of his stay.

Maize and rice can be left for days, but the opium fields were clean as gardens, the women bent-backed at their weeding and watering. They took opium to ease their monthly pains, but only the older men were serious smokers. Young Tao was sick when he tried it, then dreamt about lying in a flooded field, the water pressing its hands over his mouth, which seemed a warning against being trapped at home.

The poppies were ready, their petals falling and the bulbs turning brown. For the first time the men came to the fields. They cut each bulb with tiny silver knives and a milky liquid oozed out. That night they lay on the warm earth between the rows, talking about the days before the Revolution when China was full of poppy fields, and waking before dawn to find that the white juice had flowed all night, drying and hardening so they could scrape it into covered pots.

Young Tao left before the Chinese traffickers came. They would barter for the crop with lamp oil, cloth, iron for tools and silver for jewellery. In his last week he tried the opium again and was not so sick.

For a year he worked on the great north–south railway, with its armies of young volunteers who died in their hundreds. They built tunnels, bridges and cuttings without explosives or trucks, and Young Tao joined the abseiling squad to rest his knees, hanging on cliff-faces in a seat made of rope and bamboo. All winter he swung in mid-air heaving a pickaxe, yet the hardest trick, which took all his monastery training, was relaxing enough to release his urine.

He wanted to think about himself. Splinters bit his face and ice glued his boots to the rock while he brooded over his own popularity. He hung alongside thirty others, each hacking a cave wide enough to crouch inside, then joining the caves to make a path for wheelbarrows, and by the summer he hated them all: they liked him because he was big and a tribal and therefore easy to understand.

He came home in torn clothes and slept round the clock. He was now immensely strong – not tall, but broad as a door – so that Tao sent him with the long-nose to move a rock which was shouldering free from the hillside and threatening the terraces.

Long ago, with great emotion, Fraser had discovered the ragamuffin Scottish dandelion, growing even here. While they worked on the rock he showed little Mee Yang how Scottish children told the time by blowing on the seedhead. She ran away screaming, and Young Tao had to explain: any child knows that a dandelion seed in your ear will assuredly sprout and kill you.

Young Tao went to the docks at Shanghai, first in a factory that made sleepers and telegraph poles out of logs and tar from further up the coast, then in a gang of jolly platelayers on the dock railway, drunk together every night and the next day shovelling hard-core with a hangover, cursing these stones that lock like knuckles.

One day he walked into the university and sat solid as a Buddha through an engineering lecture. He had no rights there, but went every evening, his stinking work clothes like a uniform, so shocked by the mathematics that he had to stop working while he slept his way into this new type of seeing.

He stayed on in the railway dormitory, dozing on his cot all day amongst books he carried brazenly from the university library, tolerated by the nervous caretaker and losing his virginity to the caretaker's wife, who liked to be pinned to a wall while she beat his shoulders and demanded, in a whisper, that he stop at once. After a few months, confident of what he wanted, he enrolled full-time at the technical college in the provincial capital.

He came home and found that Old Tao was still making the same joke. He would squeeze Mee Yang's cheek and say that some husband was going to be lucky, laughing as he looked at Young Tao.

Fraser paid for Mee Yang's education and took her every day to the one-roomed school in Market Village. He held her hand as they walked along the raised track down the valley, so happy he expected to be stopped. One day on their morning walk she saw that everyone was crying, even Fraser, because Chairman Mao was dead.

During his midday rest Fraser often went again to the school-house. There was no paper on the latticed window, and he could stare inside as the children took their nap, lying in rows across the battered tables. He searched for the bundle that was little Mee Yang.

The teacher was usually dozing in his chair, but leapt up if he saw Fraser. He had hair like a Chinese peasant – dusty, and standing in a schoolboy spiral at the crown. He always wanted to talk, often about the letters he exchanged with Esperanto societies across China. Fraser almost understood them, and agreed that the language would conquer the world.

Generations of bored children had dug at the mud walls of the classroom: the teacher, whispering but angry, showed where a speck of daylight had appeared by Mee Yang's desk. Fraser promised to fix it, but disliked the man's anger and instead took pains not to wake him.

At home, Mee Yang slept in Fraser's old alcove. She became troubled by a bad dream: she was walking down the valley to school but the path became increasingly steep until she hung over Market Village as if on a great wave.

Perhaps this dream was a journey into the spirit world, thought Madame Tao. She had an instinct for such matters but was obliged to hide it from her sarcastic husband, who said that it was a great blessing that their families had been taken as slaves, because the stupid Miao superstitions had been left behind in the hills.

Madame Tao was moved that her gifts had emerged through Mee Yang, and questioned her daughter closely. At first the little girl merely remembered the dream, but under her mother's prompting the memories became more vivid. She began to relive her journey in a kind of trance.

She hated these questionings. She was aware of her mother's soft voice, but was overcome with a weakness which flooded up from her feet, making her face numb. Her lips seemed to work themselves, recounting in a sad little voice her vision of the town of monkey-spirit men.

Her mother made a fan with a little bell, which Mee Yang had to hold during her journey to the underworld. The bell signified the jingling reins of the buffalo she rode, and allowed Madame Tao to follow the child's progress: if Mee Yang paused for too long, her mother shook the fan so that the spirit buffalo moved forward again.

One morning Mee Yang wept with fear as her father left the house, and at last told him why. Tao wanted to see her performance. His wife had already invited Wang Dechen and two women from Market Village, and he was pleased at this notoriety.

In the quiet house Madame Tao began describing her daughter's journey down the valley. She was speaking to everyone but looking at Mee Yang, and told how the spirit buffalo was sure-footed on the sudden slope, and how they were now coming to the town of the monkey spirits. Mee Yang shrank back against the wall.

'They won't harm you, daughter,' her mother murmured. 'Look, they're smiling.' And indeed the monkey spirits were always friendly and high-spirited.

'They have sweets,' said her mother. Mee Yang began eating something from her fingertips. Nothing was more piercing than the sweets in the spirit town.

'And your hat, daughter.' Whenever Mee Yang came to see them, the monkey spirits gave her a hat made of beautiful feathers. Old Tao discovered that his daughter could feel nothing, not even a sharp pinch.

In her dream, the spirit town had three streets: one was full of stalls with good things to eat, another with colourful shoes. The third street was too crowded to explore, because it was market day. Mee Yang went to the one-room school. She looked in through the window: the monkey-spirit children were happy and singing, their teeth bright in the half-dark. Everywhere the monkey men were glad to see her, bowing with their fierce smiles.

Mee Yang wanted to come home, and waved the fan. She came out into the fields where the monkey boys and girls were working. They sang to her with kind voices, but she waved the fan even faster.

When she was back in the village her mother said sharply, 'Open the door, my daughter is home.' Old Tao leapt up and swept the door open, smirking as he bowed his daughter's spirit into the house.

The little girl slumped against the wall, her eyes rolled up. She was still tired when Fraser took her to school the next day. Her mother hated to see her suffer, but the vision of the spirit town was too important. After much questioning, Mee Yang sometimes saw a tall man who might be her grandfather.

The girl endured this waiting dream for some weeks, but then Fraser gave her a magazine he had found behind the hairdresser's in the town. One picture showed a beautiful blonde, her head turned away in a kind of rejection or disdain. Fraser was the first recipient of this look, during their journeys to the school, but soon the little girl used it more widely.

In particular it worked against her mother. Whenever the spirit town was mentioned, Mee Yang felt its undertow for a moment but then turned her face away and upwards in her special look.

Fraser gave her a wall mirror, which Madame Tao hated for its cold north light. Against the old woman's lifelong wish, he bought the girl a chamber pot, with a damp cloth for a cover when she carried it, head in the air, to the latrine. She had a plastic bottle of scent, which she only used if someone was watching.

Fraser gave her more magazines, scavenged from the town dump, so that the Tao house acquired a band of bright pictures around its walls, each a preferred window.

Mee was leading the dancers at the spring festival in Market Village. On her back was an embroidered baby-frame to show her readiness for marriage, though there was nobody in the valley that she would consider.

She had a wider view of the world, now that she crossed the Hog each day to the big school in town.

She had forbidden Fraser to accompany her, travelling instead with the children from Market Village. The villagers thought she should be bird-scaring in the fields, but she had her father's arrogance and didn't listen.

Fraser had made a screen of blankets around her alcove, so that she had a narrow place to dress, and every morning she cleaned her teeth with a real toothbrush dipped in a dish of salt or soot. She never left the house without her straw hat, held by a ribbon under the chin, which would make her pale as a blonde.

Today though she wore a purple hat like a stylized version of the purple turbans, but tufted with coloured scarves. She had an embroidered linen blouse with green sleeves, a black skirt and black pinafore, and pink covers for her forearms like a Victorian clerk. She held short sticks with trailing ribbons which she smacked together in time to the music, and as she danced she felt the long festival earrings swing across her lovely throat. The earrings were new, paid for by the province's nationalities committee: the funding had been arranged by Mee-Mee's former teacher from Market Village.

He was a Chinese called Tse Bri. For years he had taught standard speech to the Miao children from the valley and the surrounding hills. From time to time he was called to the Party offices and asked about disaffection among the Miao, and about the round-eye taken for a slave by crazy Tao Yumi.

He stopped teaching, became a local representative of the nationalities committee, and attended many tribal ceremonies like this Miao spring festival. Otherwise he was fully occupied in writing a report about cannibalism during the Cultural Revolution.

He was admired in Market Village. They remembered how he had cycled to the town and reported the Red Guards for destroying their paths. Nowadays, though, his popularity varied with the policies of his masters.

But there had been steadily less pressure on the old religions. He went to weddings and funerals, but only to calculate the work credits earned by the dancers, and to check that the celebrations lasted no more than ten days and that the slaughtered animals constituted no more than a third of the village stock. He always got a little drunk at weddings, because that way everything made more sense: perhaps this was the essence of the primitive mind.

The Miao were the most troublesome of tribals, but he preferred to think that this was because they were on the front line of modernity. Already clever youngsters were drawn to the mainstream, especially in accessible valleys such as this, where Miao culture would vanish in his lifetime. Young Tao might be the most successful of all, provided the opium got no worse. At least he wasn't dealing with those in-breds in the hills, still less with the thousands of Chinese immigrants in the town, riffraff shipped in from across the south-west.

But he distrusted everything the Miao told him. Lying was their entertainment. In particular he always wondered if old Madame Tao really was Mee Yang's mother, or if this was another inexplicable joke. Tao knew this and now laughed at him again.

Irritated, Tse said, 'Tell me how you murdered Huang Hua.'

Tao started talking and continued all afternoon. He admitted nothing but it didn't matter. Half the town had seen the killing, and a dozen confirmed it to Tse.

His report appeared three months later. It comprised five pages in a volume investigating all 526 of the killings in the county during the summer of 1968. Tse and his colleagues found that in seventy-five cases, internal organs had been removed and eaten.

At once a dozen arrests were made. All were senior police and Party officials, many brought back from retirement: they had betrayed the people's trust and merited the harshest penalties. There were no other prosecutions. Too many were guilty, too much time had passed, and there was anyway a reluctance to investigate the tribals: arrests could lead to discontent.

Moreover, in a handwritten note, not under any circumstances to be filed, the editor of the report had suggested: 'It is perhaps inevitable that certain low-grade Chinese are corrupted during prolonged exposure to minority cultures: in times of extreme disorder, this corruption might extend to cannibalism.'

Prosecutions, in any case, were never the point. New stirrings of political unrest had made Beijing uneasy, so it chose to denigrate that greatest of ideological disorders, the Cultural Revolution. The inquiry into cannibalism, so long after the event, was only a part of its campaign.

But Tse's report described the murder of Huang Hua and named Old Tao. What was once merely common knowledge was now official, and Madame Fei felt lashed by the insult to her family.

Tse left before the buffalo dance, which he knew by repute and which sent the unmarried women away shrieking. He had another errand in the valley. He had to cycle to the village with a message for Fraser.

There were many puzzles about the Miao, he thought, but the biggest was the round-eye. His presence near the so-called clinic was astonishing: it defied belief that he was now invited to work there.

13

Fraser took the job at the clinic. He would be the stockman, just like Old Tao years before. He thought himself lucky, because even men from the town came to ask about work, staring through the barbed wire fence at the bustle inside.

New staff streamed on newly laid paths between reopened buildings, half a dozen builders were constantly on site, and every morning trucks arrived on the river road with rats and their food. Twice a week Fraser put on a white all-over suit and fired up the incinerator to receive their grey corpses.

Occasionally he saw the pock-marked woman who had received him when he first arrived at the town. She was called Madame Fei. She was always attended by a flock of subordinates, and didn't return his glance.

But Madame Fei remembered Fraser very well. Her private laboratory held a file dedicated to him. It was supplemented with regular new entries, but one section was more than thirty years old and she used it like pornography. It was the translation of an English-language interview, and lay with related papers in a folder marked 'Application For Political Asylum: James Stuart Fraser, private, British Army'.

Interviewer: What was your tactical position.
Applicant: Beg pardon. I don't.

Int: *What was your group of soldiers doing.*

App: *Running away. I mean everybody was.*

Int: *Retreating from the Chinese advance.*

App: *Yes. But just then we were looking for some people who'd been cut off.*

Int: *What did you see at the village named Wudon.*

App: *Well. I don't know the name of the place.*

Int: *The village with feathers.*

App: *Well. I saw soldiers, sir. I think they were soldiers, spreading feathers.*

Int: *Can you hear the difference between Americans and British people.*

App: *Yes. I mean they were Americans.*

Int: *You were the last United Nations soldiers out of the zone perhaps.*

App: *Well. I think so.*

Int: *Were the Americans surprised to see you.*

App: *I don't know. They were angry, sir.*

Int: *What did they say.*

App: *Well. Nothing to me.*

Int: *You said before that they spoke.*

App: *Oh yes. To our officer. They were rude. They said to get the hell out of there. Sorry.*

Int: *How were they dressed. What uniforms.*

App: *Well, they were most of them MPs. Military Police, with white helmets. Americans. But there were some others. The others had sort of vans. A bit like ambulances but with no red crosses. The MPs just had normal jeeps. The others were wearing gloves. Well we all were. And they had parkas. Parkas. Do you know parkas.*

Int: Yes.

App: They had these steel boxes in the vans about this big.

Int: Note that the subject indicated approximately 30 by 20 by 20 centimetres.

App: And they were getting feathers out of the boxes. Handfuls. And putting them into the huts. Only they were holding them funny. I mean strange. Like this.

Int: Describe how please.

App: Well. I mean like this. Away from themselves. A bit like something smelly. Only they couldn't have smelled them. I don't think so anyway, sir. Because they were wearing these big masks. Everybody was. The MPs as well.

But not your platoon, thought Madame Fei. Which is why your comrades were no doubt inoculated as soon as they reached base, and why you almost died.

She always trembled with rage as she slid the document back into its folder. Three thousand Chinese troops had died of cholera after the United Nations retreat: once again China had been the target of biological warfare.

Even the feathers were a common thread. The Americans had taken the idea from the Japanese, who were once world leaders in bio-war, thanks to their experiments on live prisoners during their occupation of China before and during the Second World War. Some of these prisoners were Russian, British and American soldiers, but the Allies had punished no one. As in Germany, the

Americans gave immunity in exchange for the data from unspeakable research.

Madame Fei had a special passion for such matters, because she had been one of Japan's experimental subjects.

Mee Yang's schooling was over, and she worked in the fields in a Budweiser T-shirt. She dreamed of the city, where she could eat white bread and own a fashion shop.

When she was seven or eight, during one of his visits home, she had followed Young Tao everywhere, taking up the same pose, her foot on a stool or her elbow crooked. Her father had laughed and ever afterwards said that they would certainly be married. She was embarrassed and in later years contemptuous. She couldn't marry this old giant with the oily fingernails.

But at least he was free. She was beautiful, everyone said so, but must labour in this blocked valley. On difficult days, when bloody rags soaked in a covered bucket behind the screen, she blamed her parents for everything, and the valley was an infection that might invade her.

She demanded Fraser's help with a frown and accepted it without thanks, and drove even her benign father to complain: she used too much water, he said, reminding her that he had bathed only twice in his life – at his birth and his marriage – and the third time would be for his funeral.

No one understood her yearnings. She yearned like a priest or an artist for a world where the turning of a wrist or the bowing of a beautiful head could say so many, many things. But it was a cruel burden, because her art was herself and allowed no rest, no standing back, because the resting or standing back would be part of it. She bought cotton gloves, so that her hands would be pale as her face.

Young Tao, recently enrolled at the Number 2 Kunming Aero-engine factory, saw that she was still his selfish cousin but now walked as if through water, stepped up as though lifted by water, stepped down as if into a pool.

On rest days she walked to town in her yellow nylon skirt and purple nylon blouse, going first to the river to rinse her feet and put on her best sandals. She sat all afternoon in the pool room, the town's only entertainment, learning to smoke and studying the clothes on television.

She sat by the door because she was nervous, and a plump Chinese girl would join her, watching adoringly. Sometimes Mee-Mee borrowed her high heels. Boys came because she was pretty, but she was aloof, embarrassed by her Miao speech. Given time, a boy would have come who needed no replies.

Towards evening, Fraser arrived to walk her home. He had loved her since she held chopsticks in her fist not her fingers, but he was old and foreign and therefore shaming. She learned that on his way to town he checked the livestock at the clinic. She insisted on meeting him there, which is how she encountered Professor Fei.

Once a week Fraser gave blood in a whitewashed room in one of the outer buildings at the clinic. The technician hummed Hong Kong rock tunes as he filled the syringe, and afterwards gave him a small cash payment, saying, 'Hey, man.' He practised more ambitious English, disclosing such matters as the Beatles, Mrs Thatcher, and the landings on the moon.

Fraser was irritated: as usual he felt that not enough was explained. The technician didn't make clear, for instance, in what way the moon was a place.

He also heard real English, floating out of an office window. This was disturbing, because the meaning slipped straight into him as though someone had crept up to whisper in his ear. At first he hurried away as if discovered, but then he stopped to hear these words as flavourless as water, and the childish thumping music. He preferred the music of China, which is all regret.

The sounds came from Professor Fei's laboratory. Radio Beijing broadcast English lessons every day, but the Professor preferred the BBC World Service, a source too daring for all but the most established of Party members. Much important new research was published in the language, so he taped each programme and tried to fill his rest days by replaying the drab monotonous speech, which was low and hunched as its script.

He was still lonely. On rest day mornings he sat in his office, the great institution silent around him, watching Fraser arrive to tend the animals. He tried to study, but mostly worried about the weekly visit to his wife.

She lived on the top floor of the clinic, in a large apartment which the Feis had shared after their marriage. There were views to the river in front and the Hog behind, and a laboratory which she used for her private research. The apartment had been built for the Japanese chief surgeon and his family, with a soundproof double door to shield them from the slaughterhouse beyond.

Immediately through this door was a staircase down to the larger laboratory which Professor Fei had adopted for his own work. He kept his samples in drawers that still bore Japanese characters, and laid them on a zinc-covered bench whose canvas straps had restrained the surgeon's somewhat fresher specimens.

For years Professor Fei had slept on the couch in the laboratory office. At first he claimed to be monitoring certain experiments, but the arrangement had hardened into habit. Madame Fei greeted this, as everything else, with contempt. He fell asleep to a clicking in the filing cabinets, where cockroaches ate the glue from his envelopes.

Around noon on Sundays he reluctantly climbed the stairs. Madame Fei enjoyed these visits. She enquired happily about his work as they drank tea brought by the servant she called a secretary. It was part of the humiliation: she thought his ideas absurd. Occasionally she shook her head and complained about the increasing problem of space. So many new staff had arrived in the last few months: really her husband must think himself fortunate to retain his facilities.

Sometimes they saw the monkey-man Fraser in the buffalo field, and Madame Fei or her servant would remark that it wasn't surprising that a Westerner had discovered evolution. This quip was originally Professor Fei's: carelessly, he had used it more than once.

His wife so reduced him that he hated to go: leaving

would confirm his humiliation for another week. He sat all afternoon and even the servant laughed.

One week he saw a young woman from his office window. Obviously she was some creature from the hills. Her Western clothes were grotesque, but perhaps no worse than the usual Miao motley.

There was now a guard post at the main gate, and she chatted to the soldiers as she waited. They would have heard about the lecherous Miao women, that they were handsome and free, with a curl of hair at the coccyx like a little tail. The Professor, sneering from his desk, knew how the young soldiers would dream about this girl from the hills. To his amazement, she left with Fraser: she must be part of that nest of criminal degenerates in the next valley.

He began to watch for her every Sunday. It was amusing how little she moved him: one wanted, after all, some equality in a partner. She was merely pretty, but full of small-town vanity. Her face flickered between the sullen peasant, the boisterous child, and the haughty beauty, nose in the air, denying what the body promised.

He began to think of the fat Party officials with their secretaries. He was a Professor, after all, and a Party member. What was his status exactly? Would a pretty Miao be an embarrassment? Perhaps he could laugh off her folly, as a man of the world among others.

Then, to his astonishment, she appeared at his office. She was smaller than he thought, and the idiot long-nose peered over her shoulder like a dog over a bush. She simpered and bowed, but was behind it all confident, as he had seen from his window.

She wanted a job, she said. Anything, estimable Professor, because life in the fields is so hard. Fei was amazed and embarrassed, as if surprised in a crime, but promised to consider the matter. Somehow he mustered the wit to invite her back.

On the walk home Mee Yang swore Fraser to secrecy. He must say nothing to anyone about her meetings with the Professor, who would soon be her slave.

'I work all day in the fields, and come home so tired,' said Mee Yang. 'There is nothing in the village, not even a radio.'

Her face, pale as a paper lantern, was twisted with disgust. She sat self-possessed in his office. Professor Fei knew what he wanted, but couldn't see the intermediate steps.

'I want to travel. I want to go to the city. There is a shop opening in the town, selling clothes for women. I suppose you know. Perhaps you know who owns it. I want a job there. What do you think? I'm not made for the fields.'

He had made tea. Her Miao accent was awful: his name came out Fee instead of Fei. He asked her about life in the village, but knew he sounded like an indulgent uncle. His breathing was shallow, he noticed: a primitive reaction, perhaps, to the smell of strangeness. Before she left she took out a mirror and examined herself in instalments.

By their next meeting she was losing hope. While she talked, Fei looked for the marks of inferiority. The neck was a little thick perhaps, the back of the skull somewhat flat. He checked for a shadow on her forearm and lip, the hairs which are the brand of the beast, but she was perhaps too young.

The old man was useless. She mustn't waste her time. She had seen the women in their white coats walking between the clinic buildings, and pictured herself amongst them. But she instantly abandoned this dream. She took out a tiny plastic bottle, touching it to her wrists, twining her arms like amorous snakes. The smell of cheap scent filled his office.

Her contempt became anger. He was weak. What use was he. She must find a man in the town with the strength to help her. She wouldn't come again.

But Madame Fei had watched from her apartment as the young Miao came and went. She couldn't know that Mee-Mee's opinion of Professor Fei matched her own. She only saw that the clan which murdered her cousin had sent another humiliation.

Madame Fei had weapons close to hand, and was waiting when Mee Yang and the Professor came from his office – her stupid fat old husband, and this whore from the hills, handsome as the glitter on shit, her clothes grotesque as the whores who wave to the wagon drivers on the river road.

14

Madame Tao kept forgetting that her daughter was dead. The news had come after a night of fear. Mee Yang wasn't home before dark, the round-eye knew nothing, and soon the whole village was searching.

Fraser hurried over the Hog, peered through the clinic windows, questioned the fisher folk in their huts by the landing stages, and then went to the pool hall, where he was abused by a fat man in a dirty T-shirt. He returned to the clinic and banged on every door, but no one answered and again he saw nothing, not even a stray light. He went back to the village convinced she would be there, her chin lifted, refusing to see him.

Before dawn he was back in the town with Wang Dechen, hunting under the boat houses on the river. They were stopped by a policeman. He sent them to the clinic waiting room, where another policeman said that Mee Yang was dead.

It was a day of waiting. A police van arrived, and then another. Wang was sent to the village for the Taos. Fraser watched as Madame Fei and her husband came and went, and men in various uniforms held muttered conversations. He stared out of the window.

Then Madame Tao was howling in the corridor. It was the mourning cry of the Miao, which can last for days. She came in on Young Tao's arm, limp as a tragedy heroine. Her head was back, her eyes rolling, her free arm alternately beating her breast and stretched out imploringly. Fraser swallowed nervous laughter.

Madame Tao demanded the body, but a policeman said that it must be examined, as in any case of sudden death, and she returned at once to her lamentation.

They went back to the village. But the examination took some time. It would be carried out in situ, it emerged, since the incident seemed straightforward: the clinic's X-ray machine and cool store were sufficient aids, since Mee Yang had clearly died after falling down the Hog. Nevertheless, the body stayed for a month, long after the court hearing, at which her death was investigated immediately before the renewal of six market licences and just after a prosecution for drunkenness, which had involved the smashing of three windows and damage to a police officer's cap. None of the villagers went, but an account was brought by Tse Bri, who testified as an expert on Miao affairs.

The ridge was the main route between the town and the Miao valley, he told the hearing: the more direct the route, the steeper the ridge. The court was amused to learn how the Miao graded a man's health by where he crossed the ridge: the older he was, the further he walked, heading down the valley to where the ridge grew lower as it approached the river. Tse agreed that it was entirely possible that a high-spirited young girl would cross on the highest and steepest paths, even when they took her perilously close to the scree.

Instead of the Hog, the court referred to the ridge by the name given on the latest maps: it was now called Cooperation Hill, because it was a link between the

Miao and the Chinese. The verdict was death by accident.

The villagers heard nothing more until they were invited to a burial in the Chinese cemetery by the town. Beijing was ordering the people to save land by cremating their dead, so Tse Bri advised Old Tao not to protest. He was anyway too preoccupied: he would stand in the village yard, arms folded, staring towards the Hog, or sit at home with his hands on his knees, frowning at the floor like a man offered a bewildering insult.

Madame Fei came to the funeral, which was surprising and kind, but there was a distressing scene. Madame Tao collapsed at the graveside and wouldn't stay. There was much confusion. At last Young Tao, who had been holding her hand and whispering, reported that she insisted on going home: she was afraid that Mee Yang might find the house empty.

Madame Tao seemed to recover, at least in daylight. In the evenings she grew fretful. She was reliving that first night, once again angry and frightened that Mee Yang had stayed out so late. Old Tao never rebuked her but the next day she was ashamed. They had always been an ironic couple, her role being quiet amusement.

At last, holding her daughter's T-shirt, she understood that Mee Yang would never come home. She wept and was inconsolable, and Old Tao welcomed her tears.

But she discovered there were other Mee Yangs. During the day, when Tao was out, she remembered her daughter at ten years old and hurried towards the door to find her. Or she looked up from the fire, certain the toddler had chuckled in their old hiding game among the furniture: the old woman didn't search for Mee, so that all day she could feel that presence.

Madame Tao saw that she must say goodbye to a thousand Mee Yangs, and doubted her strength. Hardest of all was a half-forgotten scent. Sitting by the hearth she found that hours had passed while she drowned in the smell of babies, which is made of sour milk and warm rice cakes, and that her arm had fallen into the cradling shape.

She would let this Mee endure, she decided: the baby was so secret, no more than a shape of her lean old arm. Every day, when Tao was out of the house, she rocked and sang, cradling an old rag. Sometimes she wept but mostly she was glad, holding her daughter again.

15

Every pleasure equals its rarity, thought Young Tao, trying to be calm.

He was standing in the mouth of the cave, staring at the track from the village. It was deserted, all the way from their ragged tents to where it disappeared around a bend in the stream. When would Fraser come?

Last night the long-nose had appeared in a dream, red as a skinned dog's head. It was true that Fraser was a good man, and his friend. But his race had stolen China's ports to poison it with opium. He would say nothing to Fraser, but his anger was comforting like buried money.

Every pleasure equals its rarity: by how much he needed Fraser's urgent arrival, by so much would be the relief of his coming.

He went back inside the cave. There were only two workers now, both students from the University. Young Tao was sick of them. They laughed as they loitered in their tent, but avoided his eye when at last they emerged. They were right to be careful: his rages were a legend.

Young Tao, though, had risen early. He was unbearably restless. It was one of the symptoms, and now he hurried to the cleft and peered in. Three metres down were the bent backs of the students, silhouetted by electric lamps. They seemed to be working, crouched over their patches of lit ground, but their slow care was like a provocation. With tiny scratching and rustles they woke the itches on his back and arms.

They didn't care about the cave, but Young Tao felt he owned it, as much as the people who had lived here for fifty centuries. They had swarmed in and out of the cliff in an itch of vivid life, until an avalanche dammed the stream. A cool lake arose, deep and narrow like the pouch of a pelican. It carved swiftly through the rock fall, but the cave was choked with silt. Animals had built their burrows there, then shepherds began to clear it for a summer shelter. And at last it became Young Tao's.

He had been working at the Number 2 Aero-engine Factory, and all he could think about was his plane. He had found it in a ditch next to the airfield, rotting back to the mother, an army spotter with red stars fading on the wings. With a dozen friends he bound the rotted tyres with rope and dragged it to the factory yard.

Whenever the factory had fulfilled its targets, or had no parts or no electricity, Young Tao worked on the plane. The others came and went, playing cards by their idle machines or wandering round the town until boredom drove them to join him. They cut up a canvas chair to patch the fuselage, sealing the patches with roofing tar. They chased a shrieking mouse from the undercarriage and stole the foreman's chimney to fix the exhaust. But they were frightened of the engine because they were frightened of Young Tao.

His great shoulders, folded like a mattress, filled the engine bay. Some anonymous saint had flooded the sump with oil, but the top end was crusted with rust. He drilled out the spark plugs, solid in the rusted heads.

He bored and sleeved the rusted cylinders while the bare pistons jutted upwards for weeks, their heads drooping in a row like a mass hanging. He collected used oil and filled a tin bath, where half the engine soaked for half the winter. What he couldn't find he made on factory machines. The scent of the engine was on him like a lover's.

He still remembered the first blue spark at the plugs, and the first cough of the engine blowing straw from the exhaust. His knees flared up again, and he sought out Miao workers from the southern borders. Their opium was sticky and good, still wrapped in jungle leaves.

After six months, with a special dispensation from the company, they were given fuel for evaluation trials. On its first flight, Young Tao navigated for an army pilot, a beautiful young woman he never forgot. It was hot under the perspex, and she swept off her leather flying cap. Perhaps she was proud of her astonishing hair, which was short as a man's, shining blue-black in the high-altitude glitter.

He had taken opium and couldn't speak. He dozed behind her in the navigator's seat, glimpsing her alert eyes in the pilot's rear-view mirror. He hugged his aching knees, trying to stay awake, besotted by her yashmak eyes.

Then Mee-Mee died and he came home. In the police station yard, drug-runners had been strapped to chairs and shot in the head while local youths peered around the broken gates. So Young Tao worked in the village and amazed them with his energy. At first light he made breakfast for the Taos, who didn't speak, and then spent an hour or two in the fields before anyone else emerged. He went back to check on the Taos, then put upright sticks around the rim of his baskets so that for the rest of the day he could carry more earth. The buffalo grew nervous, circling always to face him.

But rice plants are frail in the early summer, and sluices and earth banks want nothing more than to melt back to mud. The village watched Young Tao blunder among the work of the ancestors, then told him there was nothing left to do.

So he walked tremendously. He walked to the town and came home drunk. He left after supper and woke in the hills at first light, shivering and lost. His knees swelled up again, so he sat all day on the highest point of the Hog, where he could see the town and the village and watch the riverboats vanish towards Hong Kong.

And once he followed Yi traders going home from the market in the town. He trailed them all day, punishing his knees for hurting him, and lay beside them when they camped in a cave, a giant too big to ignore or chase away. Next morning, roused by the pain, he wandered deeper inside.

A bank of silt was slumped against the back wall. Where it met the solid rock a fox had been clawing. There was a tiny hole, surrounded by bits of the herdsmen's rice. He dug with a stick until he could push his great arm all the way in. There was a cold draught, smelling of mouse. Next day he brought a shovel and uncovered a man-high opening in the rock. He crept upwards into crooked galleries.

Professor Fei travelled up from the clinic, approved

the work and left at once. Fraser came, and students were sent from the University. Boisterous and cheerful, they camped at the cave, with weekends in Market Village or the town. The government sent a little money, and Fraser was paid to bring their weekly supplies. He came drinking with them and was a great success, uncomprehending as they bantered in standard speech, but for once consenting to talk in English.

For months the galleries gave up animal bones, stone tools, and the crudest of all art – an outline of the painter's hand. They found a young stegodon, a mammal like an elephant, which had wedged itself in the narrow passages ten thousand years before. The human remains, though, were trivial. Young Tao noticed his own absorption in these scraps. He stopped thinking about the plane.

One day he paused in the entrance hall. It was wide as a railway tunnel, and he could see how the galleries would be safer. But in this period fire was a routine part of life. Larger fires, surely, would be suffocating in the closed galleries. In turn, they could make the entrance safe from predators, certainly during daylight.

Young Tao began to clear the last layers of silt from the floor of the entrance hall. At once he found dozens of hearths. Some were the faintest scorches, but others showed thousands of years of use, with compressed layers of ash many centimetres deep. Blackened animal bones and hearth stones were washed into every corner. They found a human tooth, so Professor Fei came for a week.

Young Tao set him to clear the last patch of silt.

It was close to the cave wall and he expected little of interest. The Professor worked slowly, skimming away the dirt, self-consciously careful, but could never reach the solid floor. He grew bored and drifted over to the other students, especially one bespectacled girl. He sat on his fat thighs, silent and sighing, his trowel twirling on its point like a dancer. After an hour or two he tottered away on stiff legs, lowering himself with a grunt into his lonely patch of silt.

Young Tao saw that Fei had worked the patch into a dish-shape, neglecting the edges. Clearly the silt went several centimetres below the general level of the cave floor. He sent another worker to help, amusing himself by choosing the dullest of the boys. Within a day they knew that here was an ancient fissure in the rock, perhaps as old as the cave itself. In another week, when the Professor had ceased to come, they began to discover the missing trash of the great cave.

For thousands of years its people had tossed their waste down this convenient crack. In two weeks the workers found a human femur. It had been cracked for marrow. The people of the cave had been cannibals.

Then Professor Fei was made site supervisor, despite his permanent absence. Young Tao's work had been excellent, explained the University, but the cave's obvious importance demanded a more experienced hand. Besides, wasn't he really an engineer? His friends said the University wanted a Chinese in charge, and were angry on his behalf. But Young Tao said that nothing had changed: from the start he had taken advice from the Professor.

Nevertheless he started to think about the Chinese, the Miao and whoever had preceded them in these hills. The Miao had originated by the Yellow River, far to the north. Like all the minority tribes, they had been pushed onto the worst land by the expanding Chinese. In turn, the Miao had doubtless displaced others, including perhaps the people of the cave.

Some Miao believed that the dead guarded their bones, but such ideas were dying out: Old Tao called them women's stories, foolishness for the Miao in the hills. Perhaps, likewise, such beliefs had only recently emerged, and the cave people had no such superstition. Still, Young Tao began to think that it was strange to raid the bones of these ancients for the sake of a Chinese.

Now someone was coming. It was Fraser, and at once his back ran with sweat. He hurried down the slope towards his dear friend, who would have a little package from the town, and news of his mother.

Joy had last written a decade before, saying she had heard that Young Tao's father was dead. After Mee Yang died, Young Tao wrote to her old address: Joy was perhaps Madame Tao's half-sister.

Four months later she arrived in the village, and Old Tao met her with silence: he had lost his daughter, now Joy would take his adopted son. It seemed best to move her to the town. Rooms were scarce, thanks to the new workers at the clinic, but Young Tao found a cheap place off a shared kitchen where old women gossiped all day in a fog of steam, and rubbish rotted in a puddle outside the door.

Joy had mellowed. She drifted round the town in a comfortable crouch, a cigarette in her cupped brown paws. She squinted into shops, her head thrust forward from round shoulders, and sat in tea-rooms inspecting the other clients.

She had no particular urge to talk, even when Fraser came to visit. Sometimes she met old friends in the street, but her benign calm left them uncomfortable. Perhaps she felt herself interesting after her time in the city.

For the last five years she had lived in a Guangzhou apartment block. She shared a room with two families, sleeping behind a bedsheet pinned across a corner. Her kitchen was a wooden tray propped out of the window: if it rained she couldn't cook. She worked in a noodle shop, where the customers occasionally became friends and took her home for an hour or two.

She was glad to come back up-river, where she didn't need a job and had a proper room and her own spot in the kitchen. But she was of an age to miss her roots. She found she had always hated the relentless Chinese noise, supposed to keep away evil spirits, and now there were inquisitive old women from the street committee, with hand bells and lectures about tidiness. She wanted to go back to the village.

There was a new headman. It was Tse Bri, the former teacher who had written the report on cannibalism that no one had seen but everybody knew about.

Tse was the first Chinese to live in the village. Everyone was indignant but then impressed, because he constantly tramped the hills, interviewing the oldest Miao in the most backward villages, charting their culture before it was swallowed up. Anyone could borrow his bicycle.

These hill villages had always been wretched with poverty, their people crouched on stools only a hand-span high, choking over fires of buffalo droppings and rice straw in sheds of matting and split bamboo. Now, with the easing of travel restrictions, everyone who could work had left.

Tse Bri found an old couple who knew songs from the ancestors but would only whisper, afraid of a house-hold of thuggish men, the only other villagers. In the next valley, two senile brothers slept in one another's arms in a village without roofs, tottering past him at noon to scavenge the last wormy vegetables from fields reverting to meadow. Tse Bri came home exhausted, then cycled into town to lobby for money.

His conversion had been sudden. The Miao saw all Chinese as fools, and their sniggering had always wearied him. Then Mee Yang died, and he was moved by the grief of Tao and his wife.

Shortly afterwards he was reading yet another study of Miao culture. He vaguely knew the author, a pomp-ous academic who lived with a series of very young Miao women in the hills of a neighbouring province. His study claimed to have found a village whose word for 'human' or perhaps 'the people' was close to the word 'Miao', suggesting a common origin.

He was probably lying, Tse decided: certainly it was the kind of unverifiable idea that only flourished in unfashionable disciplines like ethnic studies. But then Tse was gulping back tears, and soon afterwards volunteered for the headman's post in the village.

His interest was most convenient. The post had been empty for twenty years, ever since the stocky young man had left with the Guards for a week-long self-criticism in the town market: after this humiliation he had moved to another province, his belongings looted by the villagers and his responsibilities supposedly taken up by the headman at Market Village.

But the post could once more be funded because Fraser was once more important to Madame Fei's work at the clinic. The most significant part of Tse's duties, he was told, would be to monitor the round-eye's movements: on no account must Fraser leave the county.

So Mee-Mee was alive. Young Tao wasn't surprised. Nor that she had come to him in the middle of the night.

He lay on his cot under an old quilt in the tent he shared with Fraser. He had started to dislike the white man's smell. Madame Tao had always complained about that sweet greasy stink of mutton fat, but it hadn't troubled Young Tao until Fraser began visiting his mother.

The round-eye was snoring. He always slept well after Young Tao had been smoking. It would be embarrassing if he woke with Mee-Mee here.

She was wearing a loose robe of white linen. Perhaps she wore it when she visited Madame Tao. You never actually felt lust under opium, but a warmth was spreading over his belly. He had tried before to direct such visions. Could he make her drop the robe?

Mee Yang had been vain and silly. She would have married a young Chinese from the town, a Party member perhaps, his great joy equalling the combined regret of every man who saw her. But Young Tao could never ignore her: she had been half promised to him, and must be watched like an unlocked door.

He always lit an oil lamp when he took opium, because the soft light gave his eyes something to work on. They could build visions out of the tent fabric, which started to crawl with patterns. There were straight lines at first, so that the cloth was covered with a net or web, but if he stared at the same spot the complexity would build. There would be zigzags, then coloured patterns like Miao embroidery, then curved lines, and then ideograms that you couldn't quite read, like the writing in dreams.

Then it was wise to look away, because the patterns started to move. Grains of colour sifted over the fabric. At first they were only ants, but soon they were florid tropical creatures with many legs, and feelers that brushed your face.

Mee-Mee stood at the far end of the tent, near the flap. She had grown from a fold in the cloth. At first it was just the edge of her robe, but then a length of white leg peeked out.

The harder he stared the more she evaded him. This was a rule of opium: you couldn't examine your visions, because it took a kind of sleepiness to make them form. Young Tao let the girl shape herself out of whatever was faintly visible at the end of the tent: a patch of shadow for her black hair, a knot of tent cord for her hand holding the robe.

He wanted her to come to him. He closed his eyes, so that she could move her complicated parts. At once he heard her breathing. It came between Fraser's snores, overlapping so that he had to work hard to distinguish them.

It was a little frightening, and he opened his eyes. She had gone from the far end of the tent, leaving only the shape of her robe in the fabric. He closed his eyes again and moved his leg from under the quilt. She could only touch him gently, being a vision. Her touch would be scarcely discernible from the cool air through the tent flap. He put a hand on his lips, so she could kiss him.

Her breathing came back. There was a harshness to it now, but he would pretend this was passion. He thought he felt her robe touch his leg and then open. She kissed him, pressing harder until he felt her teeth, indistinguishable from his own. There was a bad smell, which he decided to blame on the round-eye.

But the opium had tricked him. He had closed his eyes and fallen asleep. He struggled upwards through his sleep like a drowning man, because something bad was going to happen. Mee-Mee was shaping herself in his dream, holding out her hands and weeping. She stood in the cave entrance, weeping because her hands were empty. Instead of her face there was a working blackness, eating its grief.

Fraser was woken by his groaning. He put a hand on the great chest. 'Mee-Mee is haunting us,' said Young Tao. 'We have to take her from the graveyard. We have to bury her properly, at home.'

16

'Ridiculous,' said Madame Fei.

Professor Fei was trying to study the poor finds that Fraser had brought from the cave, two bits of bone and a tooth that probably wasn't human, but his wife could not be ignored. She had taken one of the books from his desk, and sneered as she read aloud from a passage he had marked in Zhang Ziping's *Human Geography*.

' "A study of the hair and skin of our people also seems to indicate what must be considered the results of millennia of civilized indoor living. The general lack or extreme paucity of beard on men's faces is one instance of such an effect, a fact which makes it possible for most Chinese men not to know the use of a personal razor. Hair on men's chests is unknown, and a moustache on a woman's face, not so rare in Europe, is out of the question in China. On good authority from medical doctors, and from references in writing, one knows that a perfectly bare *mons veneris* is not uncommon in Chinese women." '

Madame Fei laughed. ' "Authority from medical doctors and references in writing." Yes, he is definitely a professor, I think.'

It was night when Fraser got back to the village. Down in the town, poverty was dusty and cold. Here it smelled of damp, like the cave. Fraser pushed open Tao's door and waited politely on the threshold.

'Thwa Sa!' the old man shouted, throwing back his head and laughing. Lately he had become very loud. He bustled around the firepit and seized Fraser's arm, his eyes squeezed shut with pleasure. Madame Tao looked crookedly at Fraser, and tapped her ladle on the cooking pot as a kind of welcome.

'Seng Thao's cow got in the spinach and burst itself sideways,' Old Tao shouted with delight. 'Siv Yis is pregnant again.'

'*She* is a cow,' said his wife quietly. 'Police will come.'

'Her fourth,' said Old Tao in a confidential bellow. 'And she had the third only because they found out too late.

'Perhaps your policeman will come back again,' he added, 'your good friend.' This was the usual joke about the first time Fraser came to the village, brought by the skinny young officer.

'I have been to the grave,' shouted Old Tao jovially. 'Someone has put white stones on her. Very expensive! I wish they would give the money instead to her old parents. Ha.'

Fraser, unpacking the food from town, said nothing. Madame Tao had always blamed the Professor for her daughter's death: Mee-Mee had died because of bad luck from the cave, where the Chinese dug up the Miao ancestors.

Next morning Fraser rose in the dark. He tightened his jacket as he left the village, whistling the sparrows awake until they answered. It was a day for working in the village, but first he had a secret meeting.

In the half-light, the path across the Hog was pale as a stream. Instead of going on towards the clinic and the town, he turned along the spine of the Hog. He passed between Market Village and the last of the town, descending towards the river.

Ahead was the town dump, with the black birds already circling above. But first came a dense patch of trees that held the Chinese graveyard and the resting place of pretty Mee Yang. He had come into China to be nothing and no one. Now there was this thing in his throat which wouldn't cough away.

He slanted down the side of the Hog. The town commune kept this slope for herbs, but years ago he would come to steal rabbits with Young Tao. Once the boy had brought Mee Yang on his back. She watched gravely while Fraser covered the rabbit holes with nets made from old string. Then the borrowed ferret was poured in.

In a moment rabbits were turned out of the hillside, soft as pockets. They twisted in the nets while Fraser found each neck in its bag of fur. One by one their necks clicked like a knuckle. Excited, Mee Yang put her small hands on a rabbit but it squirmed away. When she was grown, Fraser thought, he would show her how to make that soft click, more felt than heard. By then, though, she was sighing around the village, bored as a young princess. She was the princess of the village and wouldn't come.

It was still dark when he went between the white-washed posts of the cemetery, and through the trees knee-deep in mist. In Scotland he wouldn't be afraid, but he worried about the ghosts of China. They were sociable. They called to passers-by and went to dances. Sometimes, if they were beautiful in their old-fashioned clothes, young men followed them home and disappeared.

A light flickered among the graves. Fraser walked towards it and found an oil lamp in a green cup of grass. It stood next to Mee Yang's grave, which was already opened.

'Her bones are gone,' said Young Tao from the darkness.

'Oh no,' said Fraser. 'Oh no.'

The grave was a square of black that swayed like a raft. It was obvious who had taken the bones. Their fate was tied up with the clinic, and therefore with the mystery of his own presence in these secret valleys.

He glanced at Young Tao, a giant shadow among the trees, but said nothing.

For the first time Old Tao missed the round-eye. Fraser still worked hard in the fields, but he also had the part-time job at the clinic, and now this weekly journey to the cave.

He wanted Fraser near him because he had noticed his wife's secret happiness. It started a trembling, deep down, that didn't reach the surface. He had been stricken by the death of his daughter, but this strangeness in his old companion was somehow more serious. The trembling was unfamiliar but he decided it must be fear, and was a little shocked.

When little Mee-Mee was alive he had quoted an old saying against himself: 'A daughter is a happiness but a son is a great happiness.' It made him laugh because of his love for the child. But, for all his lifelong cunning, neither son nor daughter would tend his soul when he was dead. His life had been irony, which is the proof of humanity, but he couldn't laugh at the death of his daughter and his wife's madness, and this meant he would die like a beast in the dirt.

He was seventy-one years old, as near as he could tell, but declined to accept it. He walked to Market Village most rest days, and if he sat in the village yard for the rest of the week he believed it was from choice. He had grown too wise, he thought, to care about much.

He was the kind of old man he had laughed at as a boy. Every morning Madame Tao tucked him into his blue padded suit and he went first to the buffalo, regretting that nobody tended the shrine, even though the government no longer objected. Then he emptied the rat traps and laid the sleek corpses by the wall, dead but leaping, counting them with ironic sympathy, as if he too had known a cruel enlightenment.

Lastly he took the rats to the two pigs, which the village had become rich enough to keep. The old pig pen had long since disappeared, its earth walls crushed and spread on the fields, so the animals were first put in a pen made by fencing across the gap between two of the houses: Wang Dechen and the round-eye were chosen as least likely to protest.

To Old Tao's amazement, Fraser at once smashed down the fences. Snorting with joy, the pigs had rampaged through the fields, rooting up maize seedlings and the young rice, and were only caught when they stopped at Fraser's compost pit to eat the rich shit from the Party offices. They were herded into the latrine, which on reflection was the perfect place, since it was so little used. The women objected, of course, but this was no reason for the huge expense of a proper pen.

Old Tao was entirely the little old Chinaman, and Fraser stared at him with wonder. In the padded jacket his narrow shoulders disappeared, so there was a straight line from his elbows to his ears as he sat against the house wall, propped like a bundle. His walking stick stood between his splayed feet, its round handle in his hollow cheek.

He sat with Wang Dechen, whose sister was long since dead of an earache, proud because he had reached that Confucian age when desires accord with what is right. The round-eye had brought them pickle jars from the town dump and now they could drink like emperors, the lids poised in their left hands, ready to cover the hot water between sips. Madame Tao padded the jars with basketwork, trying to revive her old skill: but then she grew fretful and unpicked her work.

They were the two old men of the village, moving their chairs to follow the sun in winter or the shade in summer, watching the younger people in the fields.

They approved Fraser's handling of the buffalo, nodding when the crack of his hand reached even their deaf ears. It was the mark of a good ploughman: as the beast turned into each new furrow it received a slap to last it right to the end.

They had a lot to talk about. Tsi Bre's bicycle was the first in the village, and a couple of the younger men had already learned to ride. Old Tao squatted by it for hours, agreeably dizzy as he traced the chain around the sprockets.

And the village was full at last. Young Tao and Fraser were often away, but a family from Market Village had moved into the headman's house with their three children, so that Tse Bri lived without complaint in an old storehouse. He had fumigated both houses with hissing smoke bombs, and there was now a division between clean households and the old-fashioned ones who lived with their lice.

The new types of rice made big harvests, so there was money for fertilizer, and talk of planting winter wheat or pooling their savings to bring water from the spring in the cheap new plastic pipes. They were at last permitted to try other crops, and there were experimental stands of potatoes and barley. Most families grew tomatoes against their house-sides, and even tried the expensive fruit themselves, sprinkled with sugar, so that seedlings sprouted from the shit in their compost heaps.

Then there was Joy, Fraser's friend in the town. The long-nose wouldn't marry her, the old men agreed. Not even Fraser would want a Broken Shoe that had fitted any man's foot in half the ports on the Eastern Sea.

Young Tao gave her money, occasional visits from the round-eye would help, and no doubt there would be other callers.

'She won't need tadpoles at her age,' said Old Tao. Swallowing live tadpoles was the country way of contraception.

In the years since the last headman, Tao had led the village back to many of its habits from before the Revolution. Lately they had put throwing stones at key points among the fields, so the barbarians from deeper in the hills had to keep off their land.

The two old men watched with satisfaction as the strangers, on their way to buy and sell at Market Village, struggled under their bundles along the steep paths on the valley sides. In revenge, though, they pissed in the springs and stole the village garlic, planted in stony land above the terraces.

Only the youngest children were barefoot now, and almost everyone burned charcoal instead of coughing over damp logs. With a dozen strides, electricity poles had reached Market Village, and a bare bulb shone day and night in its main square. It was constantly stolen by other villages, who had yet to grasp its workings, and Tse Bri was pestered with questions about when the wires would climb further into the hills.

Best of all the village had a handcart, old but sturdy, which they had swapped for a pregnant sow. It had solid rubber tyres and danced at your heels like a young dog, so that one man could pull a full load to the market in the town and return the same day with light supplies.

Tao insisted that every night the steel pins were

knocked from its hubs, so that the wheels could be kept indoors. It was a risky job for Young Tao, who had to lower the axle onto a pile of logs while Fraser rolled the wheels away, but it meant that the old man could spend the evening pulling grit from the tyres and admiring the wheelwright's skill. Then Young Tao disappeared into the hills again, and when he came back there was no more talk about the wheels.

Instead, Old Tao had decorated the cart with blue, the colour of the buffalo cult, and was plaiting a shoulder harness out of old ropes, surprised that his fingers seemed weak as a girl's but without the deftness. While he worked he noticed Fraser's cool gaze and stared back in the old fearless way. But his eyebrows were white, so that he had lost his frown, and Fraser looked away only slowly.

Then Young Tao found the cave, and Fraser was gone for days at a time. Even Old Tao had to accept that Joy should move back to the village to take care of his wife. He didn't even argue when she moved in with Fraser. She was too old now to bear a half-breed.

'Did you want me?' said Fraser. 'I wanted you, but I was young.'

'I waited for you that night, and for days afterwards. I was ashamed. The village made me ashamed.'

'We were young. There was no reason to be ashamed.' They were in bed, holding hands. It was utterly dark. 'Then you were with the headman, and I was nervous again.'

'I was too unhappy. I couldn't be alone. I'm sorry. We could have been happy.'

They listened to the wind. 'We'll be happy now,' said Fraser.

Joy had stayed a few nights in her old house, for form's sake, only visiting Fraser to cook his meals. He had always eaten rice, beans, maize cobs roasted in the firepit, and something green like cabbage. These suddenly acquired spices. He liked to watch her cooking, silently honouring her travels and all she had seen in the ports of the Eastern Sea, and thinking about his own years with the Taos.

He had eaten well, or as well as Madame Tao. Sometimes there was free meat from the state, and in summer they had fresh vegetables from their private field. Naturally they both deferred to Tao. When there was meat enough for one, Tao must have it. This was usually a yellow flap, bland and chewy, that turned out to be the ear of a pig.

As with food, so with furniture. Tao had a chair, but his wife and Fraser squatted on low stools. He looked openly at them: they looked away. He farted without restraint, repeating his mantra 'Loud ones don't smell': they were discreet. He ate his lice, to frighten the rest from biting him: they cracked theirs quietly between their nails and wiped the bits on their shoes. For the first time Fraser felt a worm of anger at Old Tao. He remembered the Taos in bed, and how Old Tao had seemed deliberately loud.

Joy had brought an encrusted pan from the town. Her hands trembled as she worked over his firepit, her boxer's eyes squinting into the smoke, ash dropping from the cigarette in her brown hooked fingers. After one such meal she sat so still for so long that at last he had to put his arm around her. They lay back, staring into the roof and thinking about the lost years.

She was glad that Fraser's house had no lice. She wouldn't need the purple Miao turban which she had shed when she went to the city. Like Fraser, she grew proud of her free hair.

But he was embarrassed by her city habits. She fed the mad village cats even though they would then eat fewer cockroaches and birds. A yellow dog, the latest in a nameless series that haunted the village for a month or two until they were eaten, crept to her fingertips for scraps before resuming its distant orbit of the houses, trotting sideways as it faced the nearest human, then suddenly savage when it cornered a rat.

One of the cats permitted her caress, but was stiff as a bottle brush and would never enter the house. It sat in the hot sun by their door and lice swam like dolphins through the fur of its head, seeking the night side. It had a hidden necklace of ticks.

Their hen arrived in indignity, held by its feet like a handbag, and never recovered. Its rump pecked bare, it followed the rest of the flock round the yard, its eyes rolling as it watched the cats and picked at the bald earth.

Each evening, when the creature began grumbling

about the thickening light, Joy came to their doorway, giving her throaty chuckle when at last, flailing its clipped wings, it flew with a squawk to roost on a housetop. It preferred thatch to tile, so Fraser had to search his neighbours' roofs for its rare eggs, small as a coin, which Joy whisked with rice.

She wouldn't work in the fields, but nobody seemed to mind. She fed Madame Tao, watered everybody's tomato plants, swept the yard, repaired the latrine wall, and amazed them all by getting Fraser to bring two saplings from the hills.

She planted them on the south side of the village yard, where they would make shade trees, just like the old one from the days of slavery. She bought two of the tasteless river fish, bony as feet, and curled them through the roots for fertilizer. Behind her back Old Tao claimed the trees for the buffalo cult, pushing blue beads into the soil and rubbing blue powder on their head-high stems, though he resented the enterprise for being Joy's idea.

She had a vacuum flask, so they always had hot water, even at breakfast. Fraser could take the flask to the cave, she said, but he grew shy at such luxury and made excuses.

She sat on every threshold in the village, bringing the flask and surprising everyone with her range of flavourings. The villagers were used to plain hot water, which they called 'white tea': but chilli, mint, a musky green seed, and some blue-green leaves were tangled in a fold of newspaper in the pockets of her blue waistcoat. Her low smoker's chuckle carried across the arc of the village.

Fraser watched her from indoors, poking a tiny hole in his window-paper with a wet finger. He was always surprised when she came back to his house.

He couldn't think what she talked about with the others, because they spoke so little at home: 'Thank you,' 'I am happy,' 'I am very happy.' He was moved by this simplicity. He saw that little Mee-Mee had begun his education the first time she raised her childish arms to greet him. Now there was this choice of Joy's to turn back home every day.

There was only one disturbance in those few months. One night, lying in the dark, Fraser confessed how they had opened Mee Yang's grave and found that her bones were missing.

Joy wept, then raged against the barbarians in the hills who had stolen the bones for medicine, then told him to say nothing to the Taos. They mustn't be upset over something which couldn't be helped.

'How is Young Tao?' she asked suddenly. 'Is he still at the cave?'

'He's well,' said Fraser. In fact, Young Tao was hiding in the hills because Mee Yang kept climbing out of the crevice in the cave floor. Several times he had returned to the graveyard, checking that he and Fraser had indeed refilled her grave and that it remained undisturbed.

He had driven the two students away, and returned to the cave only to meet Fraser with his weekly supplies. Each night he tried to lose himself and Mee Yang among the stony valleys. He exhausted himself with walking, but only opium could make him sleep. As a result the girl stepped from her flesh like a bath, walking through his dreams with empty hands.

Things were also more difficult for Fraser. He had tried to remember Mee Yang as a child, but the empty grave had brought back the old confusion. She hadn't lived long enough to be kind.

He thought of the first time he had seen her, still with the birth damp on her wisp of hair, and then as an infant in the village yard in those funny toddler trousers that showed her bottom as she ran squealing after the chickens. And how later she made him say English words: 'Happy', 'Pretty', 'I love you,' and 'You are beautiful.'

Then she demanded silence. She was irritated to madness when he came to meet her on rest day evenings after the pool hall. It was for her own safety, though, and in the end she would understand. He was nervous, knowing that he talked too much: he had elected to make his lifetime confession, and told her everything – stammering, in no particular order, not knowing half the words, so that the orphanage became 'the house with the children with no mother and father'.

He kept saying something about a yellow flower, something about telling the time, but Mee-Mee knew that Fraser said flower when he meant any kind of plant. To him, rice was a flower. He said they had always held hands, and tried to demonstrate, but she shook him off with a curse.

Then he was sent away. He was forbidden to wait while she met the Professor, so each Sunday evening he loitered in the village eaten with worry. The Taos smiled to themselves: Fraser had always been a fool for the girl.

They couldn't know that their daughter visited the clinic on her way from the pool hall.

One week their smiles faded with the daylight. Fraser had known it would happen. She was staying overnight with the Professor. She had run away with him. She was on a river boat to the coastal cities because she had been kidnapped into prostitution, or had been sold in marriage to a poor man who couldn't afford a city wife, or was at last too bored to stay.

Then she was dead and Fraser thought of nothing at all. Sometimes during those months he wondered why he hadn't seen Mee Yang's body when he crossed the Hog. But after all it had been dark among the bushes.

He was silent for almost a year, sometimes suspicious but always afraid to risk his house. And there was this thing in his throat he had almost forgotten – the taste of loneliness like pennies.

Now he saw that Mee Yang's death could not be limited. She was out of her grave and tormenting Madame Tao and Young Tao, and would not be stilled until her bones were brought home.

He told Joy he would do nothing to inflame the Taos, but didn't discuss his other options.

17

'The white ones are cold and dull as the ashes of frogs, the black ones are ugly and dirty as coal.'

Professor Fei smiled over this extract he had taken from a history of British India. He was compiling an anthology of quotations from Chinese racial scientists. He wrote at the large desk in his office, so that he could spread out the dusty books which arrived from libraries throughout south China.

He was writing in the old style he had learned at school. He loved his brushes, the smell of ink blocks, and the row of characters like little houses.

'Chinese nobles are made of yellow mud,' said an undated manuscript, 'but commoners of rope.'

He turned to his selection of quotations about China's minority races, notably the Miao: like the aborigines of Australia or the American Indians, they were doomed to extinction. Such passages made his monograph unpublishable at present, but at last the truth would prevail.

'The Di people are descended from dogs, the Jiang from sheep. People who are indolent will waste away and become macaques and long-tailed monkeys,' said an early evolutionist.

His wife thought him foolish, not seeing that his paper didn't present facts but a kind of poetry. He didn't believe these early writers, any more than one believes a great play or an opera, but they displayed a truth of the heart which resonates and makes us whole. His mono-graph would show this harmony, the simple strong idea enduring as an organ note through thousands of years of Chinese thought.

Indeed, Professor Fei even included critics of his own discipline. Zhang Ziping argued in his *Human Geography* (Beijing, 1924) that skull shapes were too variable to be useful in race science. Even skin colour, that other Western obsession, was unreliable: colour was deter-mined by location, he pointed out, so that Europeans in Africa became jet black, the British in India had a yellow-blue colour and the Chinese became whiter when they moved to Europe.

Instead, said these theorists, it was hair that counted. As it grows, the human foetus retraces evolution from fish to frog to monkey, and in its seventh month loses its body hair: the Chinese, the least hairy of human races, was therefore the most advanced.

Fei had found echoes of these ideas in the most ancient texts. 'Yin is cold, female, of the earth and north: it exists to excess in reptiles,' he read aloud. 'Yang is the south, warm, light, male, active, and dominates furry and feathered creatures.'

And he had transcribed a Daoist text of the second century BC: 'The north is gloomy and dark, not bright and fresh. Its people have short necks, large shoulders, a cavity going down to the end of the spine, and cold bones. Black governs the kidneys. Its people are simple and stupid like beasts, and long-lived.'

How fertile were such ideas when set next to the

writings of Xue Fucheng (1838–1894), who believed that near the equator the *jingqi*, or vital essence, evaporated away in the heat. Only in the cool north was the vital essence congealed and thereby preserved, so that the white and yellow races were superior.

Alongside these ancient passages he borrowed from Zhang Junjun's *Reform of the Chinese Race*, which showed how the superior Chinese blood had been diluted by interbreeding with the minority tribes. Zhang advocated an Institute of Race Reform to study the ancestry of would-be mates, and prevent unhealthy marriages by segregation, exile to the borders of the empire, and ultimately castration.

'The streets are full of beggars carrying each other on their backs, tramping round hand in hand,' said Hu Buchan in his *Eugenics and Human Heredity* (1936, reprinted until 1959). 'The poorer the people, the higher their rate of reproduction.'

Professor Fei approved a recent draft law on eugenics and health which aimed to tackle the problem of inbreeding in what it termed the 'idiot villages' of China's rural highlands. He compared such modern moves with the sadly neglected Chinese Eugenics Institute (Zhongguo Yousheng Xuehui).

A baby fit for reproduction should be called 'model person' (*mofanren*), said Wei Juxian in a pre-war study, while babies bred without supervision might be called 'elimination persons' (*taotairen*) and their reproduction banned as soon as model persons made up two-thirds of the population. Wei described how the Nazis were practising 'forceful elimination' of inferior stock, but regretted their lack of determination: a much firmer hand was needed in China.

'Presumably,' Professor Fei had added in a waggish footnote, 'he later became satisfied by Nazi determination.'

He quoted Kang Youwei on racial improvement: if blacks could be prevented from eating insects or grass for several generations, at least they would lose their fishy smell. Anyone who married a black should get a medal as 'Improver of the Race'.

Professor Fei was moved by the ancient poetry of numbers. The five spices, colours, senses, metals and natural elements were matched by the five races on their five continents in the five directions – the four compass points and China at the centre. The races were like the metals: lead, iron, copper, silver, and the golden Chinese.

These images were now enriched by the Party's view of evolution, which showed that the Chinese family of races was unique, long since separated from the rest of humanity. His own studies would deepen these traditions.

Most important of all, he noted the rivalry between the yellow and white races. A school textbook from the 1920s explained: 'Mankind is divided into five races. The yellow and white races are strong and intelligent. Because the other races are feeble and stupid, they are being exterminated by the white race. Only the yellow race competes with the white race.'

Thirty years earlier, Yan Fu, himself a translator of English political philosophers, had raised the threat of extinction by the whites: 'They will enslave us and hinder the development of our spirit and body . . . The brown and black races constantly waver between life and death, why not the yellow?'

China had always been the navel of the world, but – being the Middle Kingdom – was assailed from all sides. Professor Fei ended with the clarion call of all China's race scientists. The Chinese must not be crushed as the red, brown and black races were being crushed. They must rise like the whites.

It was evening now, and he was tired. He would walk around the grounds, and then make tea and take his camp bed from the cupboard. He stood up heavily and opened the door to his outer office.

He saw Fraser, and for a moment thought that the long-nose had come to steal his manuscript.

Fraser should have been at the cave. It was his day for taking supplies to Young Tao, and he had left the village that morning with his rucksack full of treats that Joy had made for her son – sweet cakes, rice and beans, a tomato. First he went to the town: he had a sack of dried maize seeds to sell, and would buy tea and pickles for Young Tao.

He bought nothing. He sat all morning in a doorway by the market until the maize was gone, and then walked the steep alleys. For two hours he sat by the river, then went to his usual tea stall.

There were logs for seats, but he squatted at the edge of the steep lane. Its stone slabs, as big as beds, were hot through his trousers. Two old men hobbled past, each with a pig on a length of string. They were racing each other to the main square, where their animals could grub for vegetables after the market.

Fraser stood up, watched by the old woman behind the kettles, her eyes like deeper creases in her round face: he was the famous long-nose from the hills. He turned his bowl upside down on the counter and nodded with his face turned away.

He went down a side alley at random, a web of bamboo scaffolding overhead. A cat raced ahead of him, its ears pinned back. He emerged at the top of the next steep lane and stood gazing up at the clinic. He climbed halfway up the Hog, as if on his way to the cave, then lay down and slept in the sun.

He woke in the early evening. Little black flies covered the rucksack full of Young Tao's food. He stared over the town and thought about Joy, the Taos, his beautiful house and field, and the new neighbours who had filled the village. Mixed feelings were what made a home, he knew, just as mixed feelings made his life with Joy.

Lights were coming on below. It was too late to go to the cave, and now he was deliberately waiting. When it was dark he went back to the clinic. The main gate was locked beside the empty guard post, so he squeezed through the barbed-wire fence and crept in at a store-room window behind the main building.

He only wanted the bones. Perhaps he could take them with no one knowing. He recalled from his visit with Mee Yang that the Professor had a reception room, an inner office, and a laboratory. A little light from the town came in through the laboratory windows. It showed a workbench and rows of cabinets, but couldn't reach into the deep drawers where Fraser groped through a rubble of bones and rocks.

He unlocked an outside door and went to his shed behind the clinic, sitting in the gloom while a sick buffalo wheezed in its stall behind the bags of rat food. He thought back thirty years to the night when he had leaned against this shed and watched Old Tao kill the clinic buffalo. If you looked back far enough, Old Tao was always to blame.

He slept again, as a way of passing the time, then went back outside, pulling his cap down hard and straight. He left his rucksack in the shed but carried a coil of rope and the bamboo stick he used for herding buffalo. The lights were still on in the Professor's quarters, and Fraser wandered into his outer office. Then the Professor appeared.

Fraser beat him to the floor with the stick, then kicked him until he got up. The Professor raised his hands but was whipped backwards into his private office. Fraser put his shoulder to the larger man, who yielded slowly like a great door until he sat down heavily in his office chair.

Fraser took the rope from his belt and the Professor struggled again. Hot and breathless, blinded by sweat, he felt the round-eye's bony grip replaced by rope. Both men grew still.

'First you must understand the origin of the separate races,' said the Professor. He was tied in his office chair, his bare feet stretched across the chair reserved for guests. He looked like a man warming his feet at a fire, except that his ankles were tied to the chair.

There was no need for torture. He was ready to talk, blustering and afraid. The Professor had recalled a speech he gave at a dinner for some American palaeontologists, newly returned from the Gobi. Their only interest was the Jurassic and Cretaceous, but he had used the occasion to air a favourite topic. Now it was the only English that came to mind. But he had seen the blank eyes of the man with the stick, and was inclined to gabble.

'We in China have shown how the world's racial groups have been separate for a very long time. They evolved in their present locations from pre-humans who left Africa more than a million years ago.

'You Westerners disagree. You think that our common African ancestor lived only a hundred and fifty thousand years ago. If that were true, then the races would share many characteristics. We do not see any such commonality.'

Fraser said, 'I want Mee Yang,' but the Professor could omit nothing. Despite his absurd bare feet, he possessed important truths and would show this creature how superior minds had ordered his destiny, even while he struggled for decades in muddy fields.

Professor Fei quickly described a paper he had written for the academic journal *Comparative Ethnography*. Uncharacteristically it was an opinion piece. It suggested that the Nazis had made it impossible for Westerners to think clearly about race science. Westerners were especially frightened of the idea of a long period of separate development for the various races, sensing that it must raise questions about whether that development had proceeded at different speeds.

Fraser hit the Professor across the soles of his feet. Fei jerked with shock, but the blow was only a warning. The pain was still less than the insult.

Nevertheless, he paused for a moment before he could explain a further idea, one that he had not raised at the dinner for the foreign guests. It lay behind half the conversations in half the bars and buses of China, yet it was more than the Party could tolerate. It was China's equivalent of the Western fear of separate evolution.

After it had split from the rest of humanity, the Mongoloid race had itself fragmented, producing many separate sub-groups, including those apparent in China today. But the Party would not endorse an obvious truth: that the Chinese had developed furthest and fastest, with groups like the Miao retaining many subhuman characteristics.

'The minority tribes have equal rights,' said the Professor in a practised aphorism, 'but let us not confuse this with equal capabilities.'

He heard the blow before he felt it. He had time to think, 'Pain is coming,' before he was bent back hard against the chair. For a few minutes he sobbed, forgetting his dignity. His first coherent thought was wonder at this creature from the hills. How did he know it would hurt so much?

18

The Professor thought he was in a child's swing, forever swooping down and forward. Occasionally, it seemed, his feet scraped the ground. The pain was a fire in his feet and travelled on swollen wires up the sides of his neck to his ears.

In a fever, Fraser swung the bamboo lash, whipping the pale feet where sparse black hairs sprouted from the ankles. Occasionally he seized the fat neck, soft as a frog's.

Left to recover, the Professor grew maudlin, like a sad drunk. This, in the end, was why he confessed: not to avoid pain, but because pain had bewildered him. With much delay and many evasions, he described his night in the graveyard.

Her bones were grey and moist. Her flesh had melted quickly, because the soil was rich and because his wife's autopsy had been very thorough. A convenient Miao custom required a body to swiftly corrupt, so she had been buried naked in a sheet. It was fine Swatow linen, white for death, a gift from the Professor in his momentary sorrow.

He had trembled from the digging, and from the obsessive care of his excavation, more thorough than any he had done before. He worked with desperate speed, crouched in the dark with a hooded flashlight while a mountain drizzle soaked his back.

He would stain the bones with tea. Then he would take casts and return the originals to the grave.

He shovelled back the earth and was shocked at how it stood proud. But he had planned ahead, loading the clinic wagon with stones from one of his wife's interminable building works. He drove the wagon backwards and forwards over the grave, then spilled the stones onto the rutted earth.

Back at his laboratory he set the bones in a low oven, all the windows open to release the gross stench as they dried. Then at last he could sink into his chair and rest. He woke retching at noon. The room was filled with a blue haze from the oven. He took out the marrow bones, the source of the smoke, and laid them by the open window. They would take weeks to dry, and by then the bones would be back in the grave.

He laid the rest of the bones in corrosive fluid, which would eat out their fibrous content and the connective tissues which still articulated much of the skeleton. Only the white mineral form would be left: once stained the bones would resemble the ancient samples he dealt with every day. After all, he need only protect his find from brief exposure to unskilled eyes.

In the following weeks, weary and sick, flinching from real or imagined smells, he worked on the bones of pretty Mee Yang.

He measured brain capacity. It was within the norm for modern females, so he took an internal cast of the skull and examined it for brain structure, notably the degree of corrugation. There were no useful results, and he grew dizzy considering what depths of pseudo-science might come next: the angle of profile to jawline, the ratio of tibia to femur, and the size of the chin, canines and supra-orbital ridge – down and down to Victorian phrenology if needed.

He didn't make casts of the bones, nor take the originals back to the grave. His plan was absurd, he decided: he would dump her remains in the river.

This was the beginning of sanity. He started his paper on Chinese racial science and became enthused. It was a homecoming to find this community of rhetoricians, touching in their failure, who had struggled to analyse the superiority of the Chinese race even though science was as yet too clumsy to help.

Science would catch up, aided perhaps by his wife's work on genetics. Explanation and understanding must come, because the evidence was everywhere: Chinese superiority was demonstrated through five thousand years of continuous civilization. Professor Fei's work on the bones slowed and stopped. He couldn't believe he had ever thought it mattered.

Fraser gripped the Professor's ears and pulled him out of his chair. The Professor tried to walk, but fell with a groan to his hands and knees. Swinging the bamboo, Fraser drove him from the office like a beast.

Once in the laboratory, the older man hauled himself upright, leaning against the workbench, leaving red foot-prints on the concrete. Fraser tossed him the sack he had used for the dried maize. He couldn't watch as the bones were lifted from a drawer. Instead he was thinking how

Mee Yang's spirit must also have visited the Professor, until he had dug up her bones to help her passage home.

'Poison, you see,' said Professor Fei. 'Poison is the woman's weapon. And lies. It was all my wife's fault. I am very sorry.'

He knelt down carefully on the laboratory floor, then lay on his back so that the tears ran into his hair. The pain had turned his mood, and now he grieved for pretty Mee Yang, for everyone who had loved her, even for the round-eye and his years in the filthy village.

He knew it seemed like madness, his theft of the bones. But it was only a search for peace, which he hadn't known since that dreadful afternoon when his wife was waiting in the outer office.

She had run at them at once, stabbing Mee Yang with a hypodermic, shrieking that the girl was already dying, would kill anyone she touched and poison the Miao valley with her shit.

The Professor had sunk to his knees. Learning her fear from him, Mee Yang ran out. She went the wrong way, beating against locked doors, rushing along corridors, while the Professor followed in horror.

Mee Yang had slowed, as if wading into the sea. His wife dashed in little runs, issuing low moans. The Professor seemed linked to the girl, a hand over his heart while the floor took her like quicksand. As she sank, she gripped the handle of a door to the outside. He watched as she drowned, and his wife had to shriek in his face before he could stumble back to his office.

That night he had heard a noise and thought that his

wife had come to kill him. But it was the idiot round-eye, pounding at the doors, searching for Mee Yang. Professor Fei waited till he left, then went to his wife's apartment. She was awake and angry, her cigarette poised.

She issued her orders and he went into the dark and backed the clinic wagon to the door beside Mee Yang's body. He put a rope under her arms and dragged her behind the wagon – down the gravel yard, over a grassy bank and across a concrete footpath. He rolled her onto her face and dragged her back.

They lifted her ruined body onto a hospital trolley and wheeled it into his laboratory. His wife went out into the pre-dawn, and as the first light broke he saw her tiny figure coming back down the Hog, scattering certain scraps of Mee Yang and her clothing. At the bottom of the scree she paid particular attention to a large stone, smearing it with patches of the girl's scalp.

Professor Fei had smoked and trembled while his wife disappeared upstairs. After an hour he could bear it no longer and went again to her apartment. She had just called the police, she said, and now they must construct a lie. They would say they had heard the round-eye shouting for Mee Yang and had gone to help the search: they had found her body at the foot of the Hog and brought it to the clinic.

All that day, officials and hysterical Miao infested Professor Fei's office. The police chief sat and smoked at his desk, making phone calls and shouting sudden questions, but the Professor was consoled by his wife's presence and the hurried moments when they rehearsed their lie.

She faced down the police chief, smiling as she told her story, and Professor Fei thought about the moment when they would be alone and could talk again. That evening he went to her rooms but was not invited in.

He ceased his rest-day visits and continued to sleep alone in his office. He was troubled with bad dreams, but could only remember one: he had been crawling under a sheet, as if across an enormous bed, a happy sun shining down through the white linen, until he came to Mee Yang's noseless face.

One morning he woke with a kind of indignation. There was a way to settle this. It was his life's work, after all, to allocate degrees of humanity. Where else in China was a better judge of the dead girl, of whether she could grasp abstractions, and see before and behind?

That's why he opened her grave like a teeth-stealer. He must find out if she mattered. If she was less than human, then her death was less than murder.

It was light outside, and Fraser was restless. On a normal day he would be ready to work in the fields or the cave or here at the clinic. But he could see that the Professor wanted to tell him something.

At first Professor Fei couldn't speak for smiling. He could only say, 'I am thinking, I am thinking.'

He felt sleepy and comfortable. The warmth suffusing his skin no doubt marked the failure of certain vital circuits, notably the reflex that conserves body heat, but even this seemed solemn and humorous. The wounds to his head and feet warmed him like sunshine, the concrete floor was adapted to his bones.

He looked at Fraser with pity. He was lean and wrinkled, badly aged. How strange to see a round-eye dressed like a poor peasant: the cap shiny with dirt, the torn canvas shoes forever wet, the baggy trousers with layers of patches at the knee.

With amusement, the Professor noted his three jackets. Even the newest had been gone at the elbows when Fraser acquired it, and a single wooden peg replaced its missing buttons. But he wore two more, both with the sleeves torn off: one as a waistcoat, one as a kind of work coat, with layers of cloth sewn on its shoulders for waterproofing. All his clothes were grey with damp and dirt.

'You came to China,' said the Professor, his voice blurred with contentment. 'You came to China and perhaps you thought about a life in Beijing or Shanghai. You thought about young servant girls. But you came to here, to the Miao places. You lived in fields with cold water, with Neanderthal people.

'Do you ask why you live in this place?' said the Professor. 'You can ask. It is very interesting. A long time in cold water. Perhaps I will say why your life went to this rubbish place.'

The Professor smiled at an amusing idea. 'No, no,' he said, 'you should ask my wife.'

Fraser hesitated, but the Professor said nothing more, looking suddenly tired and ill. There was nothing else to do here. The Professor had pointed with his chin, so Fraser turned left outside the laboratory and followed a corridor of small offices. He came to the foot of a staircase.

It was made of varnished wood, with pictures of Chinese landscapes on the walls. A fleshy plant stood at the bottom. There was a smell of floor polish and flowers, the hint of domestic comfort.

He pushed the sack of bones behind the plant, holding down his grief. He began stepping quietly up the stairs. Behind him the Professor shouted something in Chinese.

At the top it was even more like a home. There was a small landing, with more pictures and a big pot with a painting of a dragon. He had never seen a fitted carpet: its patterned fabric bore him to a handsome door, padded with crimson leather.

He looked around, but the door was the only way forward. He paused, disconcerted by the softness underfoot like walking on a coat. He turned the handle and found a second door directly inside, propped open by a squatting brass frog.

Beyond was a corridor, bewildering with luxury. Down one side was a dark shiny table: a glossy sideboard lay along the other. Carpet had spread beneath them like a flood. On the table was a vase of fresh flowers. The wallpaper had gold stripes. This is how they live in America, he thought.

He walked down the corridor, passing open doors. One showed a kitchen with a view of the Hog, another opened into a blinding white bathroom, the third into a handsome lounge: through its wide window he could see the roofs of the town and the river beyond.

Finally, at the end of the corridor, he found a door that was closed. It was metal, painted dull red, with a rubber seal around the edge. He pushed it open and stepped into a blaze of white. He was in a short corridor, lit with fluorescent tubes, its walls, floor and ceiling clad in dazzling tiles. An air-filter whirred.

He walked to a further steel door, this time unpainted. He paused, then turned its metal lever. The door opened a fraction then stopped. He pushed harder: a heavy object slid an inch or two.

Something sprayed into his face. He stepped back, glimpsing a hand in a white glove. The door slammed shut.

He stood bewildered in the corridor. He rubbed his face on his sleeve, but the spray seemed oily and wouldn't shift. He went back to the kitchen and washed his face at the sink, fumbling for soap. He had no argument with Madame Fei. He didn't blame her for this.

He went back downstairs, collecting his sack. He didn't stop to look at the Professor, but walked directly out into the buffalo field. He stood in the dawn air catching his breath and watching the clinic for further danger.

Someone was standing at an upstairs window in one of the white all-over suits. He assumed it was Madame Fei, and they stared blankly at each other. She had given him poison, he supposed, and they were waiting for it to work.

He felt breathless, but nothing else happened. He went in to the sick buffalo. Some time during the night it had stood up. It was a fine morning and he thought the animal might do well outside.

He put on his rucksack and encouraged the animal

toward the shed door, pushing its broad haunches. He looked along its back and saw the bright sky. It was framed by the animal's black shoulders and by the doorway of the dark shed.

Madame Fei watched from her apartment as Fraser climbed the Hog. The pathogen was untried and perhaps a little too sophisticated, but she had no choice, surprised in her apartment when the round-eye entered like a husband.

She went cautiously downstairs, still wearing the isolation suit. She glanced briefly at Professor Fei, then went to his office and sat down. She wanted one of his cigarettes, but daren't take off her helmet.

Things might work out: what could be better than the round-eye convicted of a capital crime. For this and other reasons she went back to the laboratory to ensure that her husband did not survive his injuries.

She couldn't go to her apartment until it was cleaned, so she walked through the main body of the clinic and took off the suit in a sterilization room. She phoned the police, noting that this time she could more or less tell the truth. She would offer a decontamination unit to help in the round-eye's arrest.

It was still early when Fraser arrived at the village. No one saw him as he hid the sack of bones in Young Tao's house then walked on up the valley.

The sun rose as he climbed the little cliff above the springs. A first figure had emerged back at the village. Fraser thought it was Wang Dechen, and worried that he might somehow be seen. There was only one man he wanted to talk to, so he hurried on until the village was hidden.

For an hour he followed a dry valley. It seemed parallel to the main river but in fact curved slowly into the hills. This was how, all those years before, Old Tao had tricked the young policeman. Fraser crossed a ridge and followed a stream, reaching the cave at midmorning. He lay down in the tent.

At midday, Young Tao silently pressed his shoulder. Fraser sat up with an effort, unsure if he had slept. He felt sick, but went outside because Young Tao had disappeared.

It was hot, and light bounced off the rocks in the narrow valley. Young Tao stood by the stream with his face turned away, and Fraser had to go to him like a supplicant.

He could hardly speak for tiredness. He hoped for good advice, but Young Tao didn't seem to listen. He refused his mother's food with a shiver of disgust, and seemed to absorb only one part of Fraser's story: that the bones of Mee Yang were hidden under the bed in his house. He began walking towards the village.

'Wait,' said Fraser. 'I'll come with you.' But Young Tao didn't stop.

'Wait,' Fraser shouted. 'Wait. What should I do?'

Young Tao turned and looked back over Fraser's head towards the cave on the valley side: he hated this place.

Again Fraser said, 'What should I do?'

'Go,' said Young Tao, turning away. 'You should go.'

19

'I will escort you to your grave. You must stay there for ever. I will take you to the grave to be buried peacefully. You will wear shoes made of bamboo or hemp. I will wear shoes of willow.'

Young Tao was leading the Miao funeral ceremony. This part was called 'Opening the Way for the Soul to Travel to Paradise'. It was long and used archaic words, but he must make no mistakes because there was great danger. As he took Mee Yang to the ancestors, his own soul might be captured.

'If the ancestors ask who brought you, you must not say that I brought you. You must say that you came alone.

'If the ancestors ask who brought you, you must not say. You must tell them the following lie: "I have no idea who my companion was. He had great round ears like a rice winnower and eyes as big as tea bowls. He came with the clouds and disappeared with them."

'If your new parents ask who brought you, tell them that a man from the other world brought you, but because he has big hands and big feet he could not cross the river. He sank down and cannot be found again, so you are alone.

'If someone with a bad heart asks: "Who brought you here?" you must say: "Someone tall and stout." If they ask: "Can you find him?" you must say: "You cannot overtake him: his eyes are as big as a cup and his ears as big as a fan." '

After he had talked to Fraser, Young Tao had hurried back to the village. By the time the police arrived, Madame Tao had wrapped the bones in white cloth and laid them in a pot in a hole beside the fire pit.

But no one would conduct the funeral. Over the following week, Young Tao crossed the county, visiting every learned Miao, whether teacher, roadside savant, healer, part-time mystic, or supposed holy man hoarding his buried relics. All enjoyed the meeting, and talked endlessly, but they gave the same reply: Mee-Mee died young and unready, and her soul would be mad with fear and rage. At last Young Tao launched into a week-long fever to learn the ancient jawbreaking words.

'*Tog: muam xees niaj hnub, pes: nrab hnub, nplooj tsis zeeg zoo: tsis kaj, ntiaj pes teb nrag qa cai: txooj tib neeg los ntsib tuag ntim tis tag.*'

This meant: 'The day is not even the right day or the right half day. The jungle kingdom is dark and unclean. The world is full of sadness, and death awaits. The world is overflowing with all living things. That is why someone must die.'

He had already performed the chant called 'Showing the Way'. It demanded: 'Why has this person died? Who or what caused it? And do you know why there is such a thing as life and death?' It described the beginning of the world, before there was death. It explained why there is sickness and why people are born and die, and spoke of Saub, the good god, and Ntxwj Nyoog, the god of death. It reminded spirits and humans of the cycle of life, that the death of an individual is part of an endless series of reunions and separations.

'Sho-hey! Your new parents will say: "Who showed you the way here?" You will answer: "He had feet like buffalo's hooves. He took up as much room as a buffalo when he lay down."

'Your new parents will say next: "How can we follow his tracks? If we call him, will he hear? Can we catch him on horseback?"

'You must say: "He led me here this year, and left again last year. He can hear no call."'

Young Tao had learned these words from a book found for him by Tse Bri, the Chinese headman. It was transcribed from a ceremony used by a Miao tribe in the next province, and Young Tao hoped that it would be close enough to the form used in his own valley.

But the chant must be learned and not read. In the beginning, Miao wisdom was indeed written down, but on a long journey the books were accidentally steamed with rice and eaten by the buffaloes. This disaster had become legend and must not be redressed.

'Your new parents will say: "Can't we follow his tracks?" You must answer: "The weather was dry when he came. When he left it was raining and his tracks were all washed away. Partridges and pheasants scratched the ground, and leaves covered the path."

'You will say that when you came you had shoes and you crossed a bridge, but he had no shoes. He came by the mountain road and left again over the slippery rocks.

'You will say that there is no way to find the trail and go after him because he came this year and he left last year. When he came he came by land, when he returned he returned by water.

'Your grandparents will ask: "Can we ride a horse or cow to go after him?" You must answer that they can't follow him. They shouldn't follow him because they might fall into a trap. When he came the grass parted like swords and the reeds parted like spearheads. But after he left the grass closed, and the reeds will not open. You must say this so that you can meet your grandparents. Then you will let my spirit go back to the land of the living.'

The words were secret for a reason. In the beginning, the Miao were never sick. But then the Miao began to be sick and to die. They had nothing to help them, so two brothers went to Saub to ask for help.

Saub gave them four boxes. The first contained words for fun, the words spoken by a boy and a girl in love (*kwv txhiaj*). The second had the words for the marriage ceremony (*zaj tshoob*). The third had the words for a funeral (*txiv xaiv*). And the last had the magic words that would comfort people (*khawv koob*).

Saub told the two brothers, 'Keep the boxes closed. After you get home you will know which people are good and careful and have good memories. You can open the boxes and teach them the words.'

But when the two brothers got home, their neighbours took one box and opened it. This was the box of words for fun. All the people heard what was inside, and the words ran away everywhere. That's why women and men, boys and girls, all know these words.

But the wedding, funeral and magic words remain to

this day in their boxes, only taught to people who need them.

'O the dead! Now you are well dressed and you have reached the frontiers of the realm of Ntxwj Nyoog. You will climb up into Ntxwj Nyoog's territory, full of striped bamboo trees, and soon you will be one of Ntxwj Nyoog's daughters.'

As he chanted, Young Tao maintained the basic dance patterns, much simplified for his bulk and inexperience and because the dead person was not an elder. His metal necklace rang as he spun to confuse the evil spirits. He didn't perform the larger circular patterns to mimic the horseback journey of the soul: he was a little self-conscious.

'If someone finely dressed comes to show you the way, it is someone come to deceive you, and not one of your ancestors. If a person wearing coarse clothes comes to lead you, follow him, he is one of your ancestors.

'You have now arrived at your grandparents' home. Those with smiling faces and fair features who are waiting for you on the road are not your grandparents. Your grandparents are those with darker features. You can sit on their hemp skirts.

'If a spirit rooster crows and your rooster does not reply then this is not your grandparents' place. Pass on. If your rooster crows and the spirit rooster replies then this is your grandparents' place. You can sit on the edge of their coffins.'

Old Tao felt familiar to himself, back in his skin. He was still a man to whom remarkable things occurred.

Violence had been done to him and now it was balanced out. It was amazing that the round-eye had exacted this revenge, but there was a satisfaction even here: he was, after all, almost part of the family.

He didn't care about Joy. When she heard what Fraser had done, she screamed that once again her life was ruined. But she had always been trouble. She should go back to wherever she had spent the last thirty years.

The police chief was the same thin policeman who had first brought Fraser to the village, although his face was leathery with tobacco and age. He had come to the village to question them all, and talked to Old Tao for hours: he couldn't believe that the old man wasn't involved in Professor Fei's death.

They smiled briefly about old times, the policeman recalling how Tao sent him for a night alone in the hills, and Tao remembering being beaten up in the police station yard. But the old Miao told him nothing useful.

As usual, the police chief was irritated by Old Tao, who would never be punished for his crimes during the Cultural Revolution. As he rode back to town in the station jeep, he acknowledged a further cause of his anger. Old Tao reminded him of his own guilt.

It was connected to the headmaster of the big school in the town. Like all teachers, he had been at risk during the Cultural Revolution. He was put under a protective guard of his own students, but they grew bored and killed him. The police were informed, and at some point in the next two days a banquet was held at the station, where pieces of the teacher's flesh were cooked and mixed with pork.

The senior officers presided, the junior officers were ordered to attend, and drunken comparisons were made between the meat of an academic and that of a less sedentary worker. Most of the junior officers convinced themselves they had eaten only pork, but nevertheless their complicity was assured. The police chief, then a sergeant, wasn't the type for self-delusion.

He had seen Tao Yumi several times during the evening. As usual that summer he was a creature of alleys and whispered conversations, coming and going through side doors or standing in back rooms with his hands in his pockets, smiling his smile.

The Cultural Revolution had poisoned everything, thought the policeman. Millions were still sick with anger or guilt – except Tao Yumi, of course. His own career was shadowed by its horrors, his promotion accelerated when, many years later, the senior officers were instructed to resign.

They were coming to the town and he felt better. This case should be settled quickly. It couldn't be too hard to find a round-eye, who would obviously follow the river to capitalist Hong Kong.

The only awkward part was confronting Madame Fei. Whatever her part in recent events, she was still the most important person in the county. She was also the most vicious, thanks to her time being tortured by the Japanese.

20

Madame Fei had grown up during the Japanese occupation. The hairy-legs occupied swaths of northern and
coastal China, and news of their atrocities reached every
province.

At last, when Japan was fighting the Western powers,
it seemed possible to act. By then Madame Fei was a
medical student. With thirty others she formed the Patriotic Defence League of Students, and a fat ex-sergeant,
somebody's uncle, drilled them on the sports field. They
learned how to bring down telegraph poles and disable
trucks, and a friend made nitroglycerine until he lost a
hand and blew out all the windows in the science room.

In their struggle against the Westerners, Japanese
forces spread inland across the southern provinces. They
were a day's march away when the sergeant sent the
students off with a rousing speech. They were to melt
into the countryside and harass the invader.

They marched through the city, but when they
reached the outskirts all but ten had vanished. They had
brought nothing to eat, all the shops were empty, and
soon they were tired and arguing at a suburban station.
Frightened local people streamed past them onto the
packed carriages, but they stood through the hot afternoon, alternately apathetic and angry, until they were
too weary to resist the crowd.

Their train rolled through fields of tobacco and unripe

maize. Towards evening it stopped by a country halt, and the last five members of the Defence League climbed down to the trackside. The train was suddenly very tall, and their former comrades stared through the windows without expression.

It was quiet when the train had gone. There seemed to be no leader. Nervously, Madame Fei suggested they should stay by the railway: when the Japanese arrived they could sabotage the line. They began looking for a camp. It was getting dark, yet they constantly stopped to argue. By nightfall, however, they had found a barn for their base.

For three days they were happy. They had a rota for bringing water and for cooking the chickens they bought from the farmer. In the evenings they sang in the fire-light, and each gazed at the others, secretly vowing to remember.

The Japanese came on bicycles. A dozen swept past the end of the lane and disappeared. The students saw that the barn was a trap and crawled down a dry ditch to a line of bushes at the bottom of the field.

In the afternoon they watched the farmer talking to a soldier. An hour later there was a clatter of rifle fire and most of the students were dead. Madame Fei pushed through the bushes and fell onto the Japanese officer who was waiting with a pistol to cut off their retreat.

She ran on in terror, running so fast that she kept falling onto her hands and knees. Perhaps that's why she was a difficult target. She'd gone more than fifty metres before she felt she'd been clubbed.

She became confused. For days she thought that she

had done the clubbing, or was still doing it, because her back was so wrenched. But slowly the pain shrank towards her side, where a bullet had dug a ragged trench across her ribs.

As the pain left her head she found herself in an empty pigsty. After dark she was tended by the same cowering farmer who had betrayed them to the Japanese and been left to clear away the bodies. Ten days later she set fire to his house and hurried into the night, her cracked ribs jarring with every step.

She planned to travel through fields, but was exhausted by the rough ground and confused by ditches and tall crops. As night wore on she spent more and more time on the road.

The shout of a sentry was the greatest fright of her life. After that, fear became a kind of stupidity. Japanese guards shrieked at her, but she couldn't hear because of the roaring in her ears. She sat all day in a field, but learned nothing because her vision had shrunk to a patch of dirt where her hands were occasional visitors.

Pricked by bayonets she was marched towards the hills, but her limbs had thickened and she stumbled into the other prisoners. Amongst them was Chi-Chi, a round-faced girl from the League, and shame made her more aware.

They marched for three days, latterly following a river road which the Japanese were widening. The road ended at what had once been a fishing village, but was now a dozen burnt poles jutting from the shingle.

They climbed a stony slope and turned into a compound at the foot of a ridge. There were concrete buildings and glimpses of other prisoners. They spent the rest of the summer putting up more buildings, sleeping outside on bare earth and then on cold concrete behind iron doors.

When the work was almost finished she became ill. Every day a Japanese doctor examined her, while two soldiers stood guard with their unforgettable hexagonal clubs. They all wore masks. She liked the doctor and tried to understand the treatment, which was sometimes administered from a feather rubbed under her nose.

Years later, from her own file, she traced the course of her smallpox. The doctor noted that she had recovered with little treatment, and was suitable for experiments with cholera. Later he judged she would survive only one further procedure, and selected her for trials of winter clothing.

Her cell block opened into a field at the foot of the ridge. It was winter now, and every night she was dressed in Japanese combat gear and marched outside. She was fastened to a stake with fencing wire, and a thermometer, protected in a bamboo tube, was inserted into her right breast so that its bulb lay against her ribs. Records were kept of her temperature, which was taken every half hour, just before she was doused with iced water.

Like Madame Fei, Chi-Chi was young, well fed and carefully doctored by the Japanese, who were also researching cures. She too survived smallpox, although blinded, and was chosen for anthrax experiments.

The Japanese confirmed that anthrax was the most potent of germ warfare pathogens. Their prisoners died from botulism, typhus, tick encephalitis, bubonic plague, tuberculosis, dysentery, gas gangrene, influenza, meningitis, salmonella, epidemic haemorrhagic fever, smallpox, cholera, brucellosis, glanders, and the toxin of the blowfish. But anthrax surpassed them all, being sturdy, virulent, cheap to produce, and infective via the skin, lungs and digestive system.

Exposed to the air, it forms spores, whose protective coating shields the genetic material. Thereafter the disease survives in sunlight for days and in the soil for decades. After inhalation, symptoms develop within four days: a mild cough is followed by vomiting, laboured breathing, fever, aching, and collapse.

Mortality approaches 100 per cent. Its natural victims are herbivorous animals, so anthrax even has a moral force, recalling our kinship with the lower beasts.

Chi-Chi died from anthrax shrapnel. She too was tied to a stake, but in a valley deep in the hills. Her little head was protected by a steel helmet, from which a steel plate hung down over her spine. Two anthrax grenades were exploded at a range of six metres, and wounds inflicted to her legs and back. The valley had been sealed ever since.

The records occasionally referred to the prisoners as *maruta*. It was a private joke, because the word was used informally by prison staff. It meant 'lumps of wood'. The execution of prisoners who were too weak for further experiments was called 'cutting down the trees'. And 'firewood' meant corpses ready for burning, such as the little round body of Chi-Chi. There were records for almost seven hundred prisoners, but probably twice that number died before the camp was overrun by Chinese forces.

The Japanese had chosen this site because it was remote from their main settlements yet relatively secure: steep hills made it difficult to bomb and provided ramparts for their outposts. But the Chinese floated downriver on little rafts, landing at dawn and fighting uphill until they besieged the clinic.

By this time the Japanese were opening phosgene canisters in the cell blocks and igniting cylinders of chloropicrin gas. As the prisoners choked, their records were burned and the chief surgeon and his staff struggled with the more difficult task of destroying the samples in his laboratory. Nobody had time for Madame Fei.

On the ridge behind the clinic, Chinese troops had overwhelmed two machine gun nests and were filtering down the exposed slope. They saw a Japanese soldier bound to a stake, presumably as a punishment. For the moment, though, they saved their bullets for the soldiers firing from the windows.

Madame Fei had twisted herself round the stake until all but her hands were hidden from the clinic. She could see the Chinese on the Hog, and felt like a prisoner in front of a firing squad. She began to shout, knowing that the soldiers were too far to understand, but hoping they would at least recognize her as female. She shook her hair loose, and at last squirmed out of her trousers.

She was very tired. She closed her eyes, slumping forward so that her hair hung over her face and her jacket was pulled upwards. The cold-water experiments had lasted a month, and her life was no longer of interest to her. She encouraged this feeling, so that she would not be afraid or ashamed. She spread her legs.

She went back to the University. Perhaps she expected understanding, even admiration, but people only saw that she was scarred with smallpox and very angry.

The staff were carefully polite, and the male students imitated her round shoulders and tiny steps. Some of them were beautiful. You might have hoped for more from these natural aristocrats, but really they were no better than the rest, and their insults more hurtful. A woman's life was digesting all the bile she must swallow, time and again.

She stayed at the University while the Reds won the Civil War and the first minorities joined the student body. She told herself they had been liberated by Communism, the creed that would lead China to world power. But this idea became harder to maintain because they soon forgot their good fortune, and you passed them relaxing on street corners or chatting in the corridors like anyone else. There was one boy, a Yi, his wide mouth open like a frog as she lectured.

She was sent to the camp again. Supervised by the local Party, accompanied by a Japanese translator, she began her life's work on the huge medical archive left by the invader. In her free time she studied Japanese script in her room by the river, or explored the surrounding country.

It was strange to look at the camp from the ridge, or to walk freely out of its gates and down to the river:

the fisher folk had rebuilt their burned houses, but the town was still tiny – two streets on a shingle bank in a crook of the river where the Miao came to trade and the tea house stank of fish.

She worked all day at a rickety table in the archive, but avoided the rest of the camp for fear of the Japanese guards with their clubs. Her main source was the laboratory notebooks of the chief surgeon, and she could ignore their stains and smells provided the translator was with her.

This translator was a middle-aged woman who had acquired her skill before the Japanese invasion: she now worked with a scowl which was perhaps embarrassment. She missed her children in the north, and pushed her scribbled translations across the table with the briefest glance. She laced her hands and sat silently, watching for further instructions.

Each morning Madame Fei waited for her at a side door, but the woman became unreliable. Then she had to go alone to the archive. It was down a corridor with a terrifying right-angled bend, and she held her breath as if penetrating a sunken ship. She would glance quickly into the archive, praying to see the translator. If it was empty she rushed back out and kicked the grass in anger and fear.

In the end, contrary to regulations, she kept the notebooks with her. The scientific phrases were repetitious and yielded to her improving Japanese. She would sit in the tea house on the river front, eating pickled vegetables on its tiny thatched veranda and watching the riverboat coming to the concrete jetty the prisoners had built before they were sent to the camp to be killed: their bodies were burned on the town dump and the ashes thrown in the river.

The riverboat crept past her at walking pace, engine roaring, toiling upstream to the jetty. Half an hour later it drifted loose and was snatched downriver, past the fisher folk throwing their lines into the grey water, their boats tied to rocks in midstream. Then she dipped her head into a world of horror.

She went to the University to collect her doctorate and was stopped by a plump young man called Fei. He was studying palaeoanthropology and had noticed her in the town, which was surrounded by minor digs. He was a little slow, perhaps, and younger than her, but among the boisterous students he was easy company for the sour graduate of the camp.

They met again when he returned to the town. She told him she had not menstruated since her time with the Japanese. He made no comment.

In her dreams she was the skeleton she had seen by a roadside: the students were walking past, their faces turned from her nakedness. Or she was the dying Russian girl, briefly her cell-mate at the camp, who had swollen until her nipples wept and her genitals pushed outwards like an orchid.

She questioned Fei about his attitude to the tribes. There had been a fight between a local Chinese boy and three Miao. The Miao were still infected by pre-Revolutionary values, she explained. They came to the town, the men strutting, the women in their ridiculous peacock clothes. They were lazy and proud like fallen princes, and stole from the Chinese as if by right. Beyond them, deeper in the hills, were tribes sunk even further in ignorance and dirt.

Fei didn't share her passion, but acknowledged the problem. For thousands of years the Chinese had been spreading from their homeland in the north, overwhelming tribe after tribe, out to the furthest borders of Tibet and Inner Mongolia, building an empire by absorption. It was the American method, and more enduring than the overseas empires of England and France.

America had crushed its native races, but its sufferings with the blacks revealed how nations are weakened by inferior citizens. Likewise, China's tribes might linger for centuries in Darwinian twilight, debilitating the country at home even as foreigners threatened from abroad.

So he was drawn into her world view. Madame Fei reminded him of the Party line on human evolution, which declared that the Chinese race was long since separated from the rest of humanity, and therefore unique and special. He could adopt this same patriotic line, she pointed out, and thereby gain preferment.

She was right. Instead of bent-backed drudgery at remote digs, his speciality became interpreting the labour of others. Fossils and casts arrived from all across China, and he studied Western discoveries in the great international journals, questioning their dating methods and showing how the foreigners misunderstood their own finds.

They were married, and dedicated their lives to these twin threats. Fei would show how their people were unique and separate, with an inalienable right to dominate the races of China, and his wife would refine biowarfare into a weapon against the world.

She saw how it must be done. The clues were everywhere in the records.

Like the Americans in Korea, the Japanese had staged planned withdrawals during their wars in China, poisoning the land they gave up. Chinese prisoners were given bread by their captors and then released: propaganda photographs were taken, but did not show that the food was injected with typhoid, as were cakes abandoned at campsites for the delectation of local peasants.

By these and other methods, more than two hundred and fifty thousand Chinese in twenty provinces were killed by biological warfare. However, the Japanese suffered ten thousand casualties when they reoccupied a contaminated area.

Madame Fei would solve this problem of pathogens attacking their user. The issue had so far been ignored because it could only be developed by an industrialized country, and would only be used in a life or death struggle with another such country: industrialized countries were generally white.

Here though was the trump card of the Chinese. They were the only race that was also a country, the only country that could populate the earth.

Most races are vulnerable to the same diseases, but she would change this. She told her political masters of several possible lines of research, and revealed how the round-eyes were progressing with similar research: they had, for instance, infected unwitting baggage handlers at a US Navy base with *Aspergillus fumigatus*, confirming that it disproportionately hurt the blacks. She could make such pathogens more specific and more deadly.

She described other options. There could be mass immunization of China, perhaps via the water supply, before a deadly disease was released against the world. Or the immunity might be created by epidemic, as cowpox creates immunity to smallpox. She did not mention a secret hope: administrative difficulties would leave the minority tribes especially vulnerable.

Only a little further research was needed, she claimed, only some meagre few resources.

She demanded permission to begin work on Fraser, and pressed for access to the other prisoners from Korea, especially the Caucasians. The officials only shrugged and smiled. Eventually they offered her condemned Chinese prisoners, but she refused. It was trivially easy to make a pathogen too debilitated to be harmful to the Chinese: the challenge was simultaneously to preserve its potency against other races.

She reminded them how the Japanese had used white prisoners to confirm the vigour of their pathogens: the same applied even more to her own researches, where race-specific pathogens were precisely the objective.

It was grotesque that billions were spent on nuclear missiles, she said. China had too many people and not enough farmland. It would always be poor. Bio-war was the only option.

Fraser's testimony about the feathers should have settled everything. Year after year she flourished the transcript of his interview, with its first-hand evidence that the foreigners had used cholera against the Chinese in Korea. Successive generations of civil servants grew pale with anger, but again nothing was done.

By now the Feis had moved to the apartment of the Japanese chief surgeon. She liked the view from the living-room window, and stood where the surgeon had no doubt stood before, looking down over the rooftops to the glittering river. She was consoled by his great dark furniture. They bought a carpet for the stain on the kitchen floor, where the surgeon's family had been cornered by Chinese troops.

She had kept the round-eye in Decontamination as long as possible. She no longer had relations with her foolish husband, and discovered the pleasures of keeping a prisoner. Once sure of his docility she dismissed the guard and watched from the cell doorway. He was too shy to get up. He lay on the bunk, ratty black hair stuck to his forehead, his eyes darting everywhere except at her.

'Small person,' she said, knowing he couldn't understand. 'Poor person, no shoulders.' She spoke softly, a little contemptuous, as the big army boots twitched on his skinny legs. She smoked and shifted her feet.

She proposed an experiment on a tourist hotel. She would rent a room and connect a pipe to the cold-water tap from a container of pathogen. With the tap turned on and the container pumping, the water supply would be neatly poisoned. By observing the toilets it would be simple to observe how many foreigners and how many Chinese were affected.

It was crude but effective and could be repeated across the country. With a bigger pump and a more substantial access point, entire cities could be tested. Naturally, no such experiment was permitted, even though the technique had been proved by the Americans in 1945 in a New York apartment house.

She despaired. She was a mere clerk, annotating the work of the more energetic Japanese. Once again division and delay enfeebled China in its struggle against the foreigners.

In the latest journals she encountered familiar names. Dr Hisato Yoshimura, who had been in overall charge of the freezing experiments, became the first President of the Meteorological Society of Japan. On the Emperor's birthday, he was presented with the Order of the Rising Sun. He became a consultant to the trade association of the Japanese frozen food industry.

She acquired the ailments of every bio-war researcher, but more swiftly and severely because inferior safety suits and air filters meant that the clinic relied on injections and potent disinfectants. She covered her face, neck and hands with cream to replace the oils her skin no longer produced. Three times a day she took antihistamines for her growing allergies: she no longer ate eggs, milk or cocoa products. In the laboratories, a constant haze of hydrogen peroxide drifted down from automatic sprays: her skin cracked and the tips of her hair were bleached to a dirty grey. She had no sense of smell.

And the round-eyes forged ahead. Details emerged of a mock attack on San Francisco, when *Bacillus globigii* and *Serratia marcescens* were sprayed from American warships into an onshore wind. The official US report concluded that 'nearly every one of the eight hundred thousand people of San Francisco exposed to the cloud at normal breathing rate . . . inhaled five thousand or more particles'. The bacteria was supposedly harmless, but at least one person died from the *Serratia*.

She linked these experiments with the observation by US Brigadier General J. H. Rothschild of a regular airflow into China's coastal regions from Siberia and the Pacific, the latter sometimes ten thousand feet deep. She quoted his suggestion that: 'Either of these air layers could be seeded with biological agents from the air or from the water. Anthrax or yellow fever might be possible agents for this purpose.'

She would walk out into the field and wring her hands at her pitiful research facilities – this poor couple of buffaloes, the buildings raised by her fellow prisoners and now empty, and most of all the long-nose secreted in the hills but not even properly guarded, his life wearing away like her own.

The prisoners from the Korean War had long since gone home, but she demanded access to the twenty-one Americans and one Briton who had declined repatriation. Her political masters pointed out that, unlike Fraser, all these men were known to their governments. She grieved as they drifted home one by one, and something withered inside her when Fraser's fellow Briton, a marine called Andrew Condron, left in 1970.

She found another argument for the ministry. The new science of genetics was making her dream ever more attainable, she said. Soon pathogens would be made from a recipe book of genetic characteristics, targeting only certain racial groups.

She did not point out that such a pathogen might have victims among the Chinese: there was genetic diversity everywhere. In imaginary conversations she defended this sacrifice of Chinese lives. Wasn't it true, she could say, that the pathogen itself was the best definition of racehood? There was a brutal elegance here: anyone it killed was automatically an outsider. But perhaps these arguments were best presented after the event.

Race-specific pathogens were inevitable, and she felt the silent haste of government researchers around the world. As she reminded the ministry, the coming breakthrough would uniquely affect the Chinese. Such pathogens would destroy them or make them masters of the earth.

Suddenly, to her surprise, a few junior research staff arrived. There had been some invisible shift at the ministry, some change of mind or personnel, and with it a little funding for Madame Fei.

At first they merely updated the Japanese researches. A small plane was available from the army, and her team made interesting improvements to the Japanese self-obliterating bombs made of paper or ceramics. Trial drops were made along the Miao valleys and surveys made of distribution patterns.

Meanwhile there were approaches from the university, where her wilder notions could be tested. She recruited two of the students, both geneticists, and cautiously unfolded her idea for race-specific pathogens. After years of campaigning, her archive was supplemented by records from the larger Japanese camps in Nanking and Harbin, and she acquired extra translators to analyse them.

Under the cover of an aid mission, Chinese agents attended a virulent smallpox epidemic in India, and returned with samples. Through companies owned by ethnic Chinese in Malaysia and Singapore, she acquired microscopes from Russia, centrifuges from Britain, vats and drying ovens from the United States.

She was given reports from a Chinese-American agent at a California university. His department was developing pathogens which would destroy cancer cells after identifying their tumour-causing genes – a project identical to her own, except that she sought pathogens which identified race-specific genes.

The derelict clinic buildings became fermenting houses, laboratories, and live testing facilities, their staff housed in new concrete apartments in the town. She created separate departments – bacterial, viral, toxic – and, using monthly budget meetings, encouraged rivalry. She welcomed approaches from other government bureaux, and her staff made helpful suggestions about assassination techniques involving aerosols and poison pellets.

But her own research focused on the race-specific pathogens. Next to her apartment was a private laboratory which grew to occupy three large rooms, with an additional decontamination booth. Its equipment was world class: once superseded it was replaced and passed to the rest of the clinic. In particular, the isolation and sterilization procedures were such that her skin improved and her grey hairs were all natural. She was coming into her own.

Her husband's flirtation with the Miao girl – yes, that was a blow. Her own actions had been reckless and could have led to a security breach. Good fortune had been with her, even to her visit to the funeral: she had been contemplating further revenge, but the broken old couple showed that her task was done.

After all, work was proceeding well. She could watch the Miao laughing in the town and hug her secret like a lover. Further over the hills were the unspeakable Japanese.

Genetically closer to the Chinese, these two groups were issues for the future. The first target was the whites. Even a 30 per cent mortality would overwhelm them. The Chinese would replace them as rulers of the world and its inferior races.

Her motive was always fear, and the anger that grew from fear. At any time the foreigners could come again, subverting the traitorous minorities of China's indefensible border regions, occupying the giant plains, flooding up the river valleys. In the meantime, they conducted a kind of slow warfare through China's poverty. Its casualties were dead babies, millions of leaking roofs, old men sinking under their baskets by the roadside.

She could change all this. The last two hundred years would be an aberration and China would again lead the world, as it had when Paris, London and Washington were swamps peopled by savages. Her work must proceed by every necessary means.

She explained all this to the police chief on the morning of her husband's death. Ten days later, when there was no news of an arrest, she sent for him again. Fraser might be heading for his homeland, and for her own security the authorities should know what they were dealing with.

It was a hybrid anthrax, she said, which replicated only in the presence of receptors specific to the cell membranes of whites. Her pathogen took weeks to assume its full virulence against a host, but was infective within hours via the excrement, blood and nasal mucus. Its purpose was to spread widely before it was recognized.

She had intended to kill only Fraser, but if he escaped to the West it would be a great bonus. This was justice, after all. Fraser had brought news of the brutality of the white barbarians in Korea, and was returning with China's revenge.

She hadn't planned to use the weapon just yet, so it was not as discriminating as she would like, but the Chinese should be relatively resistant. And China's existing policies made it easy to seal its borders against the infection that would soon be raging outside.

Best of all, Fraser's escape meant that no one in the government had to take a decision. Only she had shown any determination over this matter. It was her initiative to keep Fraser in the hills all these years, until she had been ready for her final experiments.

'I have worked all my life to make this country safe,'

said Madame Fei, her courage growing as she spoke. 'Thanks to my work, its enemies will perish. I have given you an amazing gift, and all you have to do is let the long-nose go home.'

21

He was the only round-eye on board, but nobody noticed.

He was following the river, as anyone must, and had spent the first night among thorn bushes just downstream from the Miao valley. He had woken early and didn't move all day, watching the tugs drift past with great islands of timber from up in the hills. Towards the far bank two boys stood on the water to fish: only the wake from the tugs spoiled the illusion, rocking their little low raft.

Towards nightfall he had begun to walk. He continued until dawn, then slept for hours on a bus full of market traders and their animals. The bus stopped in a river port, and the ferry was pulling out as he leapt aboard, the passengers and food vendors throwing money and dumplings across the widening gap of water.

All afternoon he watched from under his cap as the river banks flowed past, then went ashore into crowds of Westerners.

They had a jaggedness that dizzied him. He had expected the different hair colours, but not the varied clothes that made each a stranger to the rest. Even standing in the street they were tiring as a pack of dogs – restless, looking round, with individuals leaping to the eye and then submerged. He drifted closer and heard a beautiful new word: photocopier.

In thirty-five years, he had thrown away nothing made of cloth or wood or metal, nothing that would stop a draught, patch a shirt, keep water out or in, nothing that would burn or would feed an animal or fertilize a crop. He split his matches with a razor blade, and had never cut a rope, though he had seen Tao do it, always with a flourish.

He thought he was accustomed to waste, because on the town dump he had found planks, empty tins, and the tough new plastic fertilizer bags that crazy Wang Dechen wore as raincoats, poking out holes for his neck and arms. But the Chinese were nothing to these creatures, who lived on the mere glitter of goods, shedding food or cans as soon as the gloss was gone, as if they were Miao gods, nourished by offerings which seemed untouched.

These shining strangers were the race that expelled him. He gulped a pellet of sorrow at what he had lost, and how no one had missed him.

He joined the migrant workers who camped at every railway station, the smoke of their fires making a roof across the forecourt. Washing dried on sticks pushed into the hard ground, musicians played for scraps of food, and fortune-tellers threw their beads among the restless feet.

Someone wanted to show off his English. He was a former clerk, fired in the rationalization of state industry. The young man, bitter before his time, seemed amused to find a long-nose amongst these drifting millions, but Fraser took no chances and lost him in the crowd. He remembered the clerk's sunglasses, however, and what he had said about the migrants.

He filled a plastic shopping bag with twisted newspaper to look like baggage. He took a vastly expensive train and stood in the packed corridor while a stream of urine ran from the flooded toilet. As always he wanted to merge with the crowd, and it had never been easier.

All the tribes of China were here, including strange Miao he couldn't understand. Nobody bothered him, and there was nothing remarkable about his missing travel papers. In fact there were endless good excuses for taking to the road, enough for all the homeless millions who eddied through the coastal provinces.

They were petty criminals, bewildered peasants, youngsters chasing adventure, and indignant junior officials whose cheap suits and grey leather shoes were stained with cement dust. A tide of semi-legal vagrants followed work and rumours of work, blaming their desperation on corrupt Party officials, crooked money-lenders, tax collectors with invented charges, and the capitalist roaders who left the inland provinces in poverty while the coastal regions grew fat on betraying the Revolution.

He got off after an hour, and drifted among the stalls between the tracks. Even here, miles from anywhere, there was a security check. A ragged group was handing identity papers to a guard on a concrete disc in the mud, so Fraser covered his arms, showed his bad peasant's teeth, and wore his brand-new sunglasses. This was a dangerous moment, but the guard flicked their papers back like playing cards, and enjoyed mispronouncing the stupid ethnic names: Fraser's was as strange as the rest.

Afterwards he looked again at his Chinese name, the characters clever as watch: a man walking, something like a house, a man with a stick, a ladder. They were dramatic, all exclamation marks, but now he wrote his name in the dirt, English style, like a worm.

He mouthed the words he had used thirty-five years before: 'I would like to request political asylum.'

He took the boat again, but disembarked almost at once. He didn't notice that his journeys were getting shorter. He was caught up in a jostling gang on the quay-side. Someone pushed him under a shoulder pole and he was staggered by the weight of two baskets of fish.

He followed other swaying baskets. They climbed a wooden ramp over swift water, then across a busy road and up a long flight of stone steps that were even grander than the steps to the landing stages where the Red Guards had done their killing.

He noticed another man carrying fish and followed him into a small covered market. He was a harassed stall-holder who took Fraser's baskets, then stared at him with a curse of amazement. He spilled the fish into a stone trough and pushed two coins into Fraser's hand.

Fraser went out onto the steps and looked down towards the river. He was breathless after the climb, but felt a familiar ache in his legs and a surge of pleasure like a rested athlete.

That night he slept under a bridge, hugging his new bamboo pole. His first shoulder pole had been angrily reclaimed as soon as he went back to the dock, and Fraser had shrugged and walked off, content with his two coins. An hour later he saw an unattended stall in a little street market and left its cloth roof sagging.

He had never earned money so quickly. He made a dozen journeys up the stone steps, getting lost, blundering into passers-by, slapped and jostled, but each time given a handful of coins.

Between boats he loitered with the other porters on the floating dock. They smoked, spat in the river and gossiped in a buzzing dialect which he didn't understand. They were amazed at this long-nose among them, but in the fickle way of such things decided to like him.

There was plenty of work. It was harvest time, and most of the porters had gone to their villages. For a few weeks the shopkeepers pushed money and food into their pockets, angry in their dependence, cursing the local unemployed, who said they were broke but had televisions and baseball jackets with American writing, and would rather gossip outside the employment exchange, even though there were no jobs or money, instead of working on the steps, which the town depended on.

The porters grew choosy. They turned down anything that was dirty or heavy or smelly like the fish, and only hurried when there was luggage for the expensive hotels, especially if the owners were foreign. Fraser avoided these round-eyes, content with the food markets and the small shops.

The porters were so short-handed that an old man

watched them for half a day, then started sitting on the more valuable baggage while they were off making deliveries. He had an old man's bad temper, but Fraser passed him an occasional coin, glad no longer to be the newcomer.

Fraser had a bunk in a low shed by the river. There were a dozen other men, their trades clinging to them as they rolled home each evening – vegetable porters, dockers, labourers from the fish market or the cement works.

In the bunk above him was an old Tibetan shoe-shine man who lay down each night with a long invocation to his distant gods, his kit rolled into a pillow for safe-keeping. In a dumbshow he asked Fraser's permission to pin his canvas shoes under the legs of their bunk: Fraser took the hint, so that the other men laughed because their bunk wore a shoe on each leg.

Fraser loved his job, pulling his cap down hard over one eye, which showed that the work was difficult but done with flair. Sometimes after a delivery he bought tea and a steamed bun, and leaned on his pole, one foot above the other on the steps, staring down at the river through the yellow smog.

All the life of the town had to pass him. There was a metalled road which crossed and recrossed the steps as it zigzagged up the valley-side from the river, and it was busy with roaring wagons leaving a fog of blue smoke. But the direct route was up and down these hundreds of steps, and the porters were masters here.

He bought a shirt with a rounded collar. He ate meat on rest days. He sent money to Joy, hoping she might join him. He visited every shoe shop in every alley off the steps, at last settling on a pair of black boots with thick rubber soles which the old Tibetan polished with a giggle.

In return he bought bottles of wine. On warm evenings they sat against the wall outside the dormitory, watching people go by, the old man squatting on his bundle of oils and brushes.

One afternoon Fraser didn't feel like working. He bought extra wine and they spent all day against the wall, sitting in friendly silence until the wine began to work. Then the old man sang for him. He had a breathless whine, which might have been the song or his old voice, and Fraser smiled and nodded until the wine began to work on him too.

He remembered the cruel nuns at the orphanage, and evenings round the piano. He sang 'The Skye Boat Song' while tears ran down his face. The tune was almost Chinese, he decided. Once he felt better he would teach it to the old man, and then go to Hong Kong.

The police in this town had new green patrol cars. They hated climbing the steps to check the porters, a shiftless bunch who stole even from the shops they serviced. They had been astonished to find Fraser, and had no idea what to do. The foreigner didn't have a local ration card, but among the porters this was almost normal.

However, they knew where to find him when the warrant arrived: Fraser's letter to Joy had been intercepted at the town post office. It was a great relief to the police chief with the little paunch. Fraser had proved hard to catch, because none of his colleagues down-stream believed that a round-eye could look Chinese.

Now the two young policemen laughed as they climbed the steps to arrest him. It was an enormous fuss for such a thin old peasant. They saw a grey van draw up, and soldiers in gas masks spilling out.

22

The police were cataloguing the Professor's samples. Most were resin casts, but there were a few originals, very heavy because they were partly or wholly fossilized. One sample was neither resin nor stone, and uniquely complete. Even so it might have escaped their notice, were it not for its beautiful teeth.

The police chief was wise enough to tell only Young Tao: the bones he had buried with such emotion were of unknown origin, but probably ancient. The Professor had enjoyed a post-mortem revenge.

The message came through Tse Bri, who was leaving the village. He had been missing throughout the drama of Professor Fei's murder, lost on another unauthorized tramp through the hills. He was subsequently useful in passing on village gossip, notably the story of Mee Yang's bones, which at last supplied a motive for the killing. But his obsession with Miao welfare had already irritated the local administration, and Fraser's escape made his dismissal inevitable. Nor, since the round-eye had gone, would a new headman be appointed.

Young Tao didn't mention the new bones to the family. He would go to the clinic alone and then find some secret way to bury them beside the others. He understood now why Madame Tao had drifted further into the shadows, and wouldn't leave the house where her baby needed all her care.

But Young Tao had been calmer since he conducted the Miao funeral. He had left the hills and returned to his childhood home. The cave had been abandoned: no light had been shed on the true owners of these valleys. Instead he was the water master for the village, regulating sluices, judging the level in the fields and discussing with the elders when the rice should be flooded or drained.

He was surprised by his mother's grief about Fraser. He didn't explain his role in the round-eye's departure, nor did he especially regret it, but he began to think that, given another chance, he might do things differently.

He designed a wheeled wooden frame, with a weighted lever for lifting water over the raised paths and a rope to trip the bucket as it scooped or emptied its load. He could sit down all day, working only those giant shoulders, although his knees still hurt. He took opium, cheap stuff from the hills, bought in the town from Miao he hardly knew. So far he had refused their gifts of heroin.

His opium dreams were taking him back to the old Miao ways. He had found a kind of peace there, because he saw a home for the unhappy dead. He still dreamed about Mee-Mee, Professor Fei, and other lipless creatures who wandered with empty hands or were watchful on their nest of bones, but the funeral ceremony had taught him how these spirits might be calmed.

The valley, too, remembered his recital of the Miao rites. One day, as he worked the bucket frame, two sisters from Market Village came for advice about their husbands. His reluctance to speak was impressive, and next day their mother came.

He couldn't climb the Hog now. When he learned about the bones at the clinic he had to walk the long way round: down the valley to the river road and then on to the town. The children in Market Village had found that he could be persecuted without risk. They mocked his rolling sailor's walk, and dragged down the corner of their mouths with pretended pain. Young Tao shouted, delighting them further.

There was an odd little ceremony at the clinic. A senior Party official greeted him in the Professor's old office, and a long young man stood against the wall and tried not to smirk. Young Tao was still angry, and ignored the pot of tea.

The official was fresh from a useful encounter with Madame Fei. He felt exposed by the murders. He had been the clinic's ally in the provincial government, its progress matching his own, his career advanced by every budget increase that he himself negotiated from Beijing.

The weak link had always been Madame Fei, and now she was cold with rage: the Miao valley must be cleared and its villages burned. At last he had to remind her of the unauthorized human samples they had found in a locked freezer, positioned, rather surprisingly, in her own apartment.

Madame Fei at once said that she had always worked for the good of China. Her research was progressing well. She demanded more funds.

The official appreciated her position, but pointed out that Beijing might not be so understanding. A long secondment out of the area might be best. In another research establishment she could make her unique contribution to China's security, free from painful reminders of the past.

Privately, the official believed that Madame Fei's usefulness was ending. He should have taken his warning from her murder of the Miao girl, Mee Yang, and his own hurried visit to the town. The police chief had found two soldiers as witnesses to Mee Yang's visits, and was contemptuous of Professor Fei but enraged by his wife, who seemed to taunt him with her blatant lies: serious pressure was required before he would drop his enquiries.

Madame Fei's retirement should be advanced a year or two, the official decided, after which an old age of raving presumably awaited. She was horribly scarred and crooked, thanks to the Japanese, and hadn't improved through her decades at the scene of her terror. Now age and anger were twisting her like an old root.

It was the fate of all childless women. He thought of his own son, tall and fine and doing so well in the government examinations.

He had enquired about the famous race-specific pathogen. One by one her subordinates were brought to his presence, and all behaved alike – worried, then tentative, and then covering their options. In summary: they had made little progress in such research; they doubted Madame Fei had done so; but on the other hand she was an energetic scientist who did much of her work alone.

The most useful contact had been this long young man. He was too tall to be friendly, but at last smirked and said that Madame Fei was secretive because she had no secrets.

The official was pleased at this attempt to ingratiate, but finally shrugged the matter away. He didn't believe this mad woman was capable of anything remarkable, but she would never admit that her life's work had failed, and due precautions must anyway be taken.

There was a more urgent issue. The clinic was his most important personal asset, yet for months he had been losing an argument about its location.

The town had grown enormously since the war against the Japanese. The river road had been extended upstream and rocks in the river dynamited, expanding its role as a trading centre. Hundreds of Chinese had been shipped in, and bustling alleys approached the clinic's rusty barbed wire fence.

It was an absurd site for one of China's most secret places. Foundations had been poured for its distant replacement, and he must act.

His only hope was to use Madame Fei's predicament. Instead of his present confinement in provincial administration, he could use the clinic's departure as a lever for a move to a national role. In exchange for protection from embarrassing revelations, Madame Fei could insist that she needed a familiar contact in Beijing.

'A very sad occasion,' he said to this enormous Miao. 'My sympathies to you and your family.' He wanted this over quickly. He had other matters to resolve.

'When can I see Fraser?' said Young Tao.

'Not now. Not at this moment,' said the official, taken aback by the man's size and anger.

'You can't blame him for what happened. He was traded like a slave. Anyone would be warped.'

'Of course,' said the official. 'You're quite right. And we have all been punished for it. Unfortunately, there is evidence that he made unauthorized explorations of the clinic. It was entirely his own fault, and has important implications for his own health and that of others, especially members of his own race. Naturally we can't take chances.'

'You can't stop him going home.'

'But where is his home, I wonder.'

'And you can't lock him up for ever.'

'The problem is,' said the long young man, speaking for the first time, 'there's no sure way to check for the presence of a pathogen. There are a hundred million million cells in the human body, and . . .'

'Indeed,' said the older man with a smile. 'The risk is too great. The modern emphasis is on collaboration with the West, you see. The experts tell us that if the rest of the world is desolate, so must we be. People here at the clinic had an old-fashioned view of how to improve the lives of the Chinese people.'

'You can't punish Fraser for Fei's crime.'

'The man Fraser is a Chinese citizen, who murdered another Chinese citizen.'

'Fei disturbed a grave. Insulted my cousin and the family. Fei died because . . .'

'Yes, you're quite right. And the matter will need lengthy investigation.'

'He's had a terrible life,' said Young Tao. He was remembering a time in his childhood, when he and a friend used to creep across the fields to put mud in Fraser's boots. Old Tao eventually stopped them: he said that Fraser was his property, and an insult to the long-nose was an insult to him. 'I want to see him.'

'But how can we bring him here?' The official had been startled by this giant, and perhaps had said too much, but he prided himself on rapid recoveries. 'Think of the implications for public order. And for the well-being of tourists from overseas, who will shortly be allowed free access to the county, with all the resultant increase in its prosperity. No, he must be quarantined, for the good of himself and his race. Don't you think, if we could only explain the matter, that he would want this himself?

'Even as we speak he is travelling to comfortable quarters at our research facilities in a far more secure location, where he will be under the care of my young colleague here, newly appointed as head of research.'

The young man smiled and said, 'Mongolia.'

23

Fraser is again in an ambulance, again travelling to an unexplained destination. This time, though, the ambulance is an aeroplane. It is designed for evacuations from a battlefield and can accommodate a score of patients, but Fraser is alone with his doctors. They have all-over suits like the ones at the clinic. One wears an incongruous black revolver.

Fraser is still in his work clothes, but shortly they will give him a suit made of blue paper. His cap is presently on straight, to show that he is beyond swagger, and tipped a fraction back, because he is not thinking of practicalities – but they will take that too. He stares through the tiny window, watching China for hours.

He has lived for thirty-five years among the unshiftable Chinese. In Hong Kong and Korea he touched the hem of their nation, but didn't understand. In the village, though, he bowed his head because they are beautiful as old ivory, while he is corpse-white in winter and in the summer black as dung. Only Mee Yang loved him, laughing as she tugged the hair on his arm, although her race is as old as the crocodile.

He remembers the day he came back from the Guards and found his house still empty, and the first time he bought good canvas shoes, their rope soles tipped and heeled with metal. He thinks about Joy, rising from a neighbour's threshold to turn towards his house, and the time he was working in the fields when music floated across from Market Village. In the village you never hear music, and he was drawn, still with his sickle, to watch the dancers open-mouthed. Their stage was like a house, with a roof and three walls, but more beautiful than a palace because it was made of red silk.

Now Fraser looks down at China and wonders where he is going. He expects some punishment for the business with the Professor and is content to be out of the village a little longer. He has travelled recently and doesn't mind a further adventure, as long as he soon sees his home, his fire, and Joy crouched by the cooking pots. He'll ask someone what 'photocopier' means.

It's full night now. He's surprised how few lights he can see: they must be flying over a very empty place.

It was stupid to think he could leave this country. You can't beat the Chinese. Their nation stretches round the curve of the world like a cloth drying on a rock, but dark now like a sea.

Young Tao had a rice sack. The bones were light as bread. He worked quickly, as you might hurry past a steep drop. No one must help.

'It was a terrible mistake,' said the official. 'One madman.'

As usual, his young colleague was silent. He was thinking how Madame Fei wasn't wrong, only premature. She had been right, too, about the value of a deniable Caucasian. Before his own career was over, perhaps some use might even be made of Mee Yang's soft tissues, also safely journeying north.

Blind, Young Tao stumbled outside. Crowds filled the streets, but it was dark and the sack of bones looked like a sack of tools. When he reached the river road he laid it softly over his shoulder.

Mee Yang was lighter than the day he had carried her to catch the rabbits. The bones lay companionable against his back as he started the long walk home.

AFTERWORD

All the authorities quoted in this book are genuine, from the Chinese racial theorists to the US Brigadier with his observations about useful air flows into China. The Miao funeral ceremony really is this impressive, and yes, some Chinese believe that whites have four testicles.

Real China, by John Gittings of the *Guardian*, was my initial source on cannibalism during the Cultural Revolution. Mr Gittings was kind enough to read this book in manuscript. Like him, I've found many incidents too gruesome to describe, but have used the geography of Wuxuan, scene of the most extensive of these atrocities, for my fictional Chinese town by a river. A fuller account of these horrors is contained in Zheng Yi's book *Scarlet Memorial*.

Like the West, China has a long and squalid tradition of racial pseudo-science, some of which is quoted in Professor Fei's paper. Unlike the West, where the awful example of the Nazis is more immediate, these theories retain respectability.

The Chinese, for example, still flirt with eugenics, that British-born science of regulating human reproduction for the good of the species. As the book notes, a draft law was recently formulated for the suppression of 'idiot villages' in the rural highlands: deliberately or not, such a law would bear most heavily on the tribal minorities. These themes are explored in several works by Frank

Dikotter, notably his *The Discourse of Race in Modern China*, to which I am deeply indebted: I am honoured that Professor Dikotter has placed *Something Like a House* on the reading list for his students at the School of Oriental and African Studies, the only novel to appear there.

And Chinese Communists have indeed adopted the evolution theories of the pre-Revolutionary government. We could charitably attribute this to intellectual conservatism, but their notion of a long separation of the human racial groups is also convenient for an ancient nationalism. Genetic research, however, increasingly supports the majority Western view that the races, including the Mongoloids, are so similar that they must have separated rather recently.

This same research will identify increasing numbers of the DNA segments which produce racial characteristics. This in turn will make race-specific pathogens ever more easy to design. In June 1997, US Defense Secretary William Cohen warned of 'types of pathogens that would be ethnic specific so that they could eliminate certain ethnic groups'. He declared that 'the scientific community is very close to being able to manufacture' such weapons.

In January 1999, in a report called *Biotechnology, weapons and humanity*, the British Medical Association said that within 'five to ten years' it would be possible to manufacture 'genetic weapons which target a particular ethnic group'. These weapons would develop from two apparently benign research endeavours: the Human Genome Project, which aims to map the entire human genetic make-up; and gene therapy, which uses biological agents to introduce DNA into diseased cells.

The BMA, which represents all British doctors, added that there is no theoretical obstacle to the creation of 'viral vectors or micro-organisms' capable of attacking one genetic group while sparing its neighbours.

At its Ness Ziona germ warfare laboratory to the south of Tel-Aviv, Israel is allegedly engaged in the difficult task of developing such weapons for use against the genetically similar Arabs. More direct evidence exists of similar ambitions in the old South Africa: in testimony to the country's Truth and Reconciliation Committee, a former senior agent of the apartheid regime recalled his search for a pathogen capable of 'only making sick and killing pigmented people', on the grounds that curtailing the black birth rate was the regime's 'most important task'.

There is evidence that the Chinese have a current germ warfare programme. In his memoir *Biohazard*, the Russian defector Dr Ken Alibek, formerly deputy head of the Soviet Union's main bio-war research agency, reveals, 'In north east China, [Soviet] satellite photos detected what appeared to be a large fermenting plant and a biocontainment lab close to a nuclear testing ground. Intelligence sources found evidence of two epidemics of haemmorrhagic fever in this area in the late 1980s, where these diseases were previously unknown. Our analysis concluded that they were caused by an accident in a lab where Chinese scientists were weaponising viral diseases.'

For China's earlier experience of germ warfare, this book draws most heavily on *Unit 731*, by John Williams and David Wallace. The Japanese Army group named in the title carried out dreadful bio-war experiments on its prisoners, including Britons and Americans, yet its members went on to comfortable careers in post-war Japan, thanks to a familiar exchange of data for amnesties.

Nor was Japan the last to use the Chinese as targets for germ warfare. In his eye-witness account of US troops emptying boxes of feathers in a Korean village, Fraser is no more than a mouthpiece for the testimony of a real-life British soldier, a sergeant in the Middlesex Regiment interviewed by Williams and Wallace.

In short, China has unique experience of bio-warfare. As Madame Fei suggests, the Chinese would also be wise to consider themselves unique as possible victims or exploiters of race-specific pathogens: nowhere else is there such a precise coincidence of racial and political boundaries around such a colossal population.

On a far lighter note, Sarah Lloyd's shrewd and beautiful *Chinese Characters* was the most evocative of the travellers' memoirs I read. The Miao funeral service was compiled from translations by Symonds, Geddes, Falk, Chindarsi, Lemoine, Schworer Kohl, Clarke, Tapp and McNamer.

The theme of this book is race, but I would never suggest that bigotry is especially prevalent in China. The country's constitution and legal code are in general admirably liberal, even though, as elsewhere, these high principles break down in practice.

Racial distinctions take an unfamiliar form in China, but no accusation could be more self-defeating than to claim that a race is racist.

A HOUSE BY THE RIVER

Sid Smith's stunning second novel, *A House by the River*, is also set in China. This sneak preview of an opening chapter displays his trademark mix of adventure, lyricism and intellectual daring.

The river flows for a thousand miles across south China. It rises in the outposts of the Himalayas and struggles for half its length among the gorges and rapids of the foothills. Hundreds of miles from the source it is still violent and cold where it passes a gravel beach.

Downstream the river escapes the hills. Its torrent is soothed in China's subtropical plains and at last enters the ocean in the great delta whose folds enclose Canton and Hong Kong. But here at the beach its broad back is lumpy as cable and leaps over upjutting rocks.

Fisher people founded the town. They came from the lowlands, where the river is warm and shows a man's reflection, but had been spreading upstream for generations, until the river grew talkative, then bared its teeth among the rapids of the uplands. At last they reached a rapid where the foam leapt like fish among the boulders, so they turned their boats, riding back on the swift current until they came to the beach.

At first they only camped here, sleeping for a summer night or two under mat shelters. But they saw how the river slowed a little because it curved around a headland of harder rock. On the far bank, this curve undercut steep mountains, whose scree slid into the water. On this side, though, in the lee of the little headland, the river was calm and dropped its gravel.

They brought drying racks from their settlements

downstream: while they fished, an old man stayed on the beach, chasing away foxes and river birds, turning the catch in the sun and covering it during the thrashing summer storms. He buried fish offal in the gritty soil above the beach and grew a few vegetables.

A steep slope climbed from this beach, covered with thin earth, thorn bushes and tufts of grass. It levelled into a stony meadow then reared into a great ridge, restless with sliding gravel, the first arm of the mountains.

Tribespeople watched from this ridge. They were jealous of the boats, made of hardwood from downstream, and decided they were being robbed of fish they could not catch. Each winter they took anything the fisher folk had left, even the fertilized earth, which seethed with insects and steamed in the cold air as they dug.

One summer they painted their faces and raided the drying racks, stealing half the catch while the old man ran into the shallows and the fisher folk rowed desperately to shore. Next season the fisher folk camped off the far bank, sleeping in their boats tethered to half-submerged boulders, drying their fish on poles wedged into the grey scree, in terror of the rocks which tumbled from above.

The old man took charge and a trade began. The tribes acquired the fish in exchange for game or for the crops they raised around their own summer camps, though the barter was conducted with grunts and mime and much suspicion.

The fisher folk returned to the beach and raised their

improbable platforms, twice as tall as a man, which swayed above the shallows on driftwood poles as thin as a wrist. There was a floor of matting, a mat roof, and one mat wall which was moved to face the wind but taken down when the wind grew too strong, lest the whole trembling contraption should founder. Fishing lines trailed from the platforms into the deeper water, and at night the boats were drawn between the drift-wood poles, and a bed made there for their owner, because they were more precious than any habitation.

There was still talk among the tribes that the fish should be paid as tribute for the use of their beach. But by now the fisher folk were staying through the winter, when snow in the mountains ceased to melt and there was less water to hide the fish. Although the fangs of half-submerged rocks became more numerous, the water was so tame that even the tribesmen took to their clumsy rafts, although they disliked the river, which crossed their land like a foreign army and was too cold to touch. The fisher folk, too, had lost their downstream affection for the river, and forgot how to swim.

The houses of the fisher folk moved to the shingle, acquiring thatched walls and hunkering down on shorter, stronger poles. Women appeared around the houses and were carefully observed by the tribes, who had ceased to resent the fisher folk, only bad-tempered old men recalling that the beach had once been theirs.

The fisher folk caught all the fish in the shallows behind the headland, dipping their bamboo scoops into the slick water, or casting their nets, so they moved into the midstream, which was too deep and fast for nets and scoops, except perhaps during the winter drought. Instead they grew adept with hooks and occasionally spears.

The fish of the midstream were big from fighting the current. A man might catch nothing for days but when he trapped one of the midstream fish, dragging it to the beach behind his boat then leaping into the water to club it to death like a man, he could eat for a week.

Fish are formed out of bubbles from the bottom of a river, like the bubbles in a swamp. Downstream, fisher folk honoured the river for its muddy fecundity, because the fish were anonymous and unending. But here the great clean fish had to be defeated one by one, and the fisher folk shouted and sang as each was wrestled ashore, strong as a leg. They swapped tales of their catches and grew contemptuous of their cousins downstream, who had to boil their drinking water and could hold a rod in each hand because the fish were too small to fight or, if they were big, seemed in recollection to have watery flesh or be diseased.

The old man died and was launched into the river in a fishskin cap, his wrists and ankles tied, his mouth sewn shut around his one treasure, a silver fish hook which would pay the fish god for passage to the underworld, or (some said) would convince the god that he was only a dead fish.

The fisher folk explored upstream. They went on foot because the river was too violent even for their skill, adopting an old tribal path which wound among rocks on the river bank, wary of tigers and the poison darts of the tribesmen, launching fishing lines from tiny beaches, or dropping them into the mist from the walls of thunderous gorges, or balancing into midstream across slimy boulders to drift them into deep pools at the foot of rapids.

Young men went furthest. A few penetrated to the river's source and saw it vomited from the womb of a grey dragon which had been cursed for fighting the fish god. But all of them saw the logging camps where the raft men began their journeys, and found them run by the local tribes with the raft men feted as their hardiest warriors, who rode the vicious river and brought back cash, which was rare among the mountain people and could be given to monasteries.

One such monastery stood among its graves in a quiet side valley, so far upstream that it lived on tribute from Tibet, whence it had been carried by dragons two thousand years before. Some of the young fishermen learned that they were reincarnations of dead monks and stayed for ever, becoming will-less as water, finding themselves through obedience, as water does. But the rest came back to the shingle beach, because at last even young men cease to feel misunderstood.

During China's troubles the Emperor's grip loosened on the outposts and the river people almost forgot him, absorbed in their struggles with the river and each other. In times of peace his influence was renewed. A tax collector visited the area but his levies were disappointing. The fisher folk, used to paying land tax downstream, were no trouble. But the tribespeople merely lifted their mat houses and moved to another valley.

However, taxation meant protection, so the Yi people began discussions with the collector. The area had been too unsettled for farming, but certain assurances were made and an opium plantation appeared in the valley next to the town, with a Yi farmer and his family and slaves.

This valley lay behind the great ridge above the beach. It had its own stream, fed by reliable springs whose clear water grew muddy in irrigation channels among the poppies, at last entering the river downstream from the beach.

At first the plantation had only a handful of slaves, mostly Miao, who worked in the poppy fields alongside the Yi and were well-treated and allowed their own rites at marriage and death. But still they tried to escape, and this ingratitude brought overseers with whips to patrol the edge of the fields: at night the slaves were shackled in houses that had to be as strong as the master's. These expenses could only be recouped in one way: more slaves were acquired and the Yi no longer learned their names.

The valley passed to the farmer's sons and grandsons, so that for generations there were three families side by side, which was all the valley could support. Occasionally the storehouse was looted by drunken tribesmen, but Imperial troops staged punitive raids and the problem eased, though there was always petty theft from the fields.

But the thin soil of the plantation was growing exhausted. The Yi growers were removed from the worst pressure of the Imperial government against opium, which is anyway very profitable, but they grew poorer and blamed the slaves.

So instead they became a power in the land. They lent money to the local tribes and took young people as security: often the youngsters were forfeit and sold up-river to cousins of the Yi. They allowed a market to be set up in summer and charged the stallholders. The customers were mostly tribals, who disliked the beach over the ridge with its tax collector and fights with the fisher folk.

The Yi built a stone storehouse on the riverbank near their settlement and, for a small rent, donated its use to the boats which collected their opium. A fat man sat by its door smoking his wages – a few balls of opium – and trading salt, sugar and tobacco for the poor goods of the tribals, who came to the port from far upriver and far inland, carrying furs, dried meat and the medicinal parts of bears and tigers, squatting for days with a peasant's patience, waiting for the riverboat whose schedule they could never understand.

Their trading done, they lingered outside the storehouse licking rock salt, and at last reluctantly picked up their bags, now full of salt, knives and needles, and climbed into the hills in single file, taking a final look at the hardwood boats that were curved like the eaves of temples: upstream there were only rafts, used as fishing platforms or for crossing streams, though landlords and rich monks sometimes had planks laid on inflated pigskins, drawn by their retainers, naked in the icy water.

The riverboats went no further. Luxuries for the tax collector were carried by porter to the beach of the fisher folk, who were themselves content to walk to the river port for their small needs. And upstream of the fisher folk settlement were the serious rapids: mere sails and oars and poles could not counter their violence, and even the great gangs of coolies who hauled the riverboats through the downstream rapids would have strained and cursed and torn their bare feet and finally lost the boats to the river god.

By then the Yi settlement was known as Market Village, and was bigger than the fisher folk camp on the beach. Young men from the fisher folk visited on market days and during the festivals, feeling themselves dull besides the bright clothes of the Miao women and the luxuries of the Yi slave owners, their silver necklaces and wine, and humbled by the strong Yi houses, even though they were built on the ground where animals and dirt could come in. On the way, they bathed in the icy river to remove the shameful smell of fish, then sang in the moonlight as they stumbled home drunk across the steep ridge, which they called the Hog – an auspicious animal to which it bore no resemblance.

So the beach of the river folk was eclipsed. A tottering wooden jetty was built into the water to save the silk robes of the tax collectors, and a little shed, with no windows and an earth floor, housed the three soldiers who comprised the collector's bodyguard. Next door, a wooden house, carried upstream in sections every year, sheltered the collectors from the summer rains, though not from the stink of fish.

One collector was called Hoo Fat. On a warm day in spring, relaxing on his veranda overlooking the river, he opened a package of official papers, newly arrived on the riverboat.

He was startled to read that his soldiers must leave the old house with the wooden floor. In future it would be home to two white people.